Ghosts
in the
Graveyard
Texas Cemetery Tales

Olyve Hallmark Abbott

Republic of Texas Press
Plano, Texas

133.122
abb

Library of Congress Cataloging-in-Publication Data

Abbott, Olyve Hallmark.
　　Ghosts in the graveyard: Texas cemetery tales / Olyve Hallmark Abbott.
　　　　p.　cm.
　　Includes bibliographical references and index.
　　ISBN 1-55622-842-2 (pbk.)
　　1. Haunted cemeteries--Texas.　2. Ghosts--Texas.　I. Title.

BF1474.3.A23　　　2001
133.1'22--dc21　　　　　　　　　　　　　　　2001031966
　　　　　　　　　　　　　　　　　　　　　　　CIP

Republic of Texas Press is an imprint of Wordware Publishing, Inc.
No part of this book may be reproduced in any form or by
any means without permission in writing from
Wordware Publishing, Inc.

Printed in the United States of America

Photos by author except where otherwise noted.

ISBN 1-55622-842-2
10 9 8 7 6 5 4 3 2 1
0107

All inquiries for volume purchases of this book should be addressed to
Wordware Publishing, Inc., at 2320 Los Rios Boulevard, Plano, Texas
75074. Telephone inquiries may be made by calling:
(972) 423-0090

Dedication

To the memory of my parents, Hamilton and Survella Shults Hallmark, and to Tom Abbott, good spirits, all. For my sister Billie Mills and my daughters, Devon and Taryn.

Contents

Contents

Acknowledgments

During the last year many generous people have shared their intriguing stories with me. Without their help, I would not have had a ghost of a chance to complete this book.

My gratitude goes to Robyn Conley-Weaver, author and leader of the Fort Worth Writers Group. Her friendship and endless support kept me digging up more haunted graveyards. The special members of the writers group have offered constructive comments at our weekly meetings. It's about time I thanked them again!

Special thanks to my sister Billie who ventured with me into the wilderness to take pictures, reminding me to hold my camera steady and not to step on the cactus.

I extend my appreciation especially to Kimberly Olsen and her mother Joyce Olsen, Charles LaFon, Eric and Linda Archer, Nancy Robinson Masters, Nichole Dobrowolski, John Troesser, Ralph Wranker, Katie Phillips and Pete and Carolyn Haviland.

My warm regards go to Ginnie Bivona, my editor at Wordware's Republic of Texas Press. We agree that a sense of humor is the best medicine of the day—that, and chocolate.

Introduction

When I began researching material for this book, many ghostly tales presented themselves without much effort on my part. Collecting them would be a breeze. Serious-minded, respected, reliable, and sensible people discussed the paranormal with me. Considering that description, when they told me their experiences in connection with cemeteries, I felt my own skepticism drift away like a gossamer mist.

Soon, however, I realized I needed more stories and went out into the field myself. Make that out into the cemeteries. It was certainly a hands-on experience.

If I didn't find a country graveyard in the daylight, I'd not find it after dark. Unless, of course, a glowing tombstone lit the way. And twice, they served better than flashlights.

Having a career in television and theatre, the only ghost I was familiar with up until now was "The Ghost of Banquo" in Macbeth. Still, I'd rather see than be one.

During one of my searches on a 109-degree Texas afternoon, grasshoppers stalked me as I located certain gravestones in Wise County. At least I think that was a grasshopper on my shoulder.

I pleaded for eerie tales from members of organizations I belonged to and contacted friends from my Southern Methodist University address books. Then I set out in my car (with maps carefully marked and enlarged).

I stopped in wonderful small-town libraries, barbershops, newspaper offices, the Chambers of Commerce, and yes, even doughnut shops early in the morning. I purchased more apple fritters than I ate, but I obtained good tales from locals who drank coffee and chatted about their regional ghost stories.

Everyone seemed interested in contributing to this collection. If they didn't know a story, they had a telephone number handy of someone who might.

The day I came home from Grand Saline, the town had a flood like it hadn't had in years. Just after I visited the cordial town of

Mineola, fire destroyed several downtown businesses. Throughout the course of writing these stories, a perfectly healthy pecan tree in our backyard split in half, the garbage disposal came to a grinding halt, and the clothes dryer dried its last tennis sock.

I choose to believe my writing a ghost book had nothing to do with any of those occurrences. This is a friendly book, and I hope ghosts everywhere will think kindly of my writings. I would be delighted if one showed up for a book signing—and I wouldn't sign with disappearing ink.

Read the tales with an open mind. They are for pleasure, a bit of paranormal significance, a little seriousness, and hopefully a laugh or two. If you are a nonbeliever in the supernatural, you may change your mind, unless your skepticism is etched in stone. Then again I've learned nothing is etched in stone forever.

Chapter 1

Ghosts in a Cemetery?

"Beware ye who pass by
As ye be now so once was I
As I be now so must ye be
Prepare for death and follow me."

~18th Century New England Epitaph

What better place for a Texas ghost hunter to find ghosts than in a cemetery? Prior to the twentieth century, the term was graveyard, which sounds more somber, more haunted.

What *are* ghosts? Some people believe them to be unhappy spirits of the dead. That lets Casper out—he's downright gregarious. Usually, these spirits are unaware they are supposed to have died, or at least do not accept it. However, if a ghost had a tragic or particularly untimely death, it may want to stay around, thinking it can somehow make things right—whatever is "right" to a ghost.

Nevertheless, a ghost is a hazy apparition of a departed loved one, or it *may* be a loved one. Others seem to be happy to go about their own way when mortals venture by. They have reportedly been dressed in their period clothing and walked through doors, windows, and trees. Motion pictures have proved that, haven't they?

References are made to phantoms, ghosts, demons, specters, and apparitions—illusionary images? Chances are a friendly ghost would not choose to be called a demon, which runs the gamut from devil to vampire. Of course, a little demon might be an imp and that can't be too bad.

My husband proposed marriage to me while parked at White Rock Lake in Dallas, bringing out three engagement rings so I could have my choice. That's why I paid little attention to the strange lady in a beautiful white dress who knocked on our car window. I did notice her dress was wet. But I had more important things on my mind. The story about the rings is true. It's up to you whether or not to believe the part about the lady knocking on our window.

Thus far, the only ghost I may have come close to was the Lady of White Rock Lake, but the book isn't finished yet. She supposedly had an argument with her sweetheart. After leaving a party, she drove her car into the lake and drowned. She still wanders around stopping cars to ask for a ride home, leaving only a wet spot from her dripping gown on the car seat—after she has disappeared.

Some people say a ghost exists to avenge a crime or to right a wrong. A spirit of a murder victim might return to cause trouble for his killer. Other ghosts may believe if they cross over, away from life on earth, they will leave something undone. They resist the move until they set things straight. Others may simply like it here, with a curiosity to see what is going on around them.

One story is of a young woman from East Texas who lost her two children in a fire. After her own death, she has been seen carrying buckets of water to put out the smoldering embers.

Rumors of ghostly apparitions are a part of our history. For centuries, tens of thousands of people in all the world's cultures have reported seeing ghosts in different forms. Ghosts play a part in many primitive religions and have been favorite subjects of storytellers and writers. Shakespeare must have felt strongly about them when writing *Hamlet* and *Macbeth*. And Marley's ghost in Dickens' *A Christmas Carol* caused us to think about the supernatural when we were children, as our children do now.

Ghosts have been reported as appearing in different forms. Up until recently I thought an orb was an eye. I never knew it is a transparent ball of electromagnetic energy... er, ghost? An orb can be round, or if it is moving swiftly, it blends into an oval shape, tapering at the end in a tail-like fashion. They may appear in odd shapes as well but tend to show up in photographs as round balls of mist.

How do you know when you have seen a ghost? Perhaps you have never seen one. Perhaps you have felt only its eerie presence in the form of a brief but definite chill, like walking into a cold spot on a warm day. A wisp of cold may brush against you and before you can turn, it's gone. The hairs on your arm may rise or your nerve-endings race to join each other. Be alert for such an omen during an evening cemetery visit.

Whatever "spirit" crosses your path, be it a weird sound, a strange sighting, or a cold spot, it is still an unexplained phenomenon. The ghost of Great-grandpa Zeke from Bonham may have merely wanted to say hello and tell you that even if he did steal a horse, it was a fine animal.

A common belief is ghosts appear more often at night when light is poor. Our senses can play tricks on us when we can't see so well. Moonlight casting its glow through the trees can be interpreted as a ghostly creature. Then, perhaps it really is a ghostly creature.

No one knows when or where a ghost will appear. You may never experience seeing, feeling, or hearing one, but you can enjoy reading about them.

Remember if a misty orb shows up on one of your snapshots taken in a cemetery, it does not necessarily mean a water spot was on your camera lens.

Ghosts have been documented over the ages in houses, inns, on bridges, under bridges, in palaces, lakes, trains, and cemeteries. And haunted cemeteries are what this book is about.

While reading these tales, keep the following terms in mind:

- ✧ Apparition: A strange or supernatural sight or thing.
- ✧ Ectoplasm: A supposed emanation of a materialized spirit to which spiritualistic phenomena are attributed. A form of spirit energy appearing as white swirl-a-gigs or as a vapor.
- ✧ Ghosts: The disembodied spirit of the dead, emerging to the living as a filmy illusion or apparition. What most of us

call a ghost, scientists call an "entity." According to Dr. Dave Oester and Sharon Gill, authors of *Twilight Visitors*, "Ghosts are the mirror images of their mortal life, just without the body." They tend to cling to life in our dimension. Most of the time they do not know they are dead.

✧ Orb: Perhaps no one knows the true definition of an orb, in the paranormal world. Orbs are not visible to the naked eye. An orb appears as a transparent circle or oval, and is said to be spirit energy when captured on film. We see them on many photographs of graveyards and other haunted places.

✧ Spirit: A spirit can manifest itself anywhere and knows full well it has passed on/over/up/down. It may just return for a visit to know what's happening, like seeing if the stock market is better or worse since he/she became a spirit.

✧ Phantom: Heard, seen, or sensed, but having no physical reality; appearing only in the mind.

✧ Poltergeist: Responsible for disturbances usually taking place in houses or buildings, but not always. Items are moved, drawers pulled out, and objects tossed askew. Lights go on and off, not because of normal electrical problems. Usually connected with a young girl.

✧ Shade: A term for ghost.

✧ Wraith: A ghost of a person just before death.

✧ Will-o'-the-wisps: Even though they appear to be of paranormal nature, the wisps are really phenomena made of natural gas. Hovering over swampy areas, they move as we move, causing us to think they are following or at least moving alongside us.

✧ Vortex: In the world of ghosts, a vortex is a whirling column of white ectoplasm-like material. Some photographs have shown it to be blue-white. Also, in a photograph, it can be mistaken for a camera strap, except when the camera *had* no strap.

I am not an expert on the paranormal. I am a storyteller. The definitions are to help out with your reading. But if you see any of the above in a haunted graveyard, feel free to call it anything you like. Just say a prayer and whatever you do, be nice.

Chapter 2

North Texas

Deep Creek
(Ssh!)

If you would like to join my friend Virginiae and me on a visit to a haunted bridge and a very old cemetery, come along. We may get lost, but at least I'm a safe driver. And while we're so close to Aurora Cemetery in Wise County, we'll check that out, too.

Deep Creek Cemetery and "Whispering Bridge," as some have called it, are on the outskirts of Boyd, Rhome, or Aurora. The latter's skirts are closer if you're driving from Fort Worth as we are, although Deep Creek is recorded as being in Boyd. First, we'll leave Fort Worth on 287 north, then turn west on 114 to Aurora.

Only the cemetery and a few houses are left to remind us a community called "Deep Creek" ever existed. It was thus named for its steep banks when the first settler built a house nearby.

We have now turned west on 114 and Aurora is just up ahead. Times have changed. The town is active once again.

It isn't easy to see FM 4227, but now that we've spotted it, we're turning north. We should be at Deep Creek Cemetery in four miles or so. I guess it could be simple to miss...No, it isn't. There's a sign. "No Trespassing." Oh!

The heavy iron gate is carefully designed, as well as locked, so no one should enter without permission. Yes, all those horizontal spikes pointing forward on the gate would take care of the "carefully designed" part, as well as the front of the car, should someone force an entry.

At this point on a 109-degree September afternoon, it looks as if an army of grasshoppers is all that's needed to ward off intruders. We can stalk grasshoppers the same as ghosts, although I've never had a ghost land on my shoulder—or have I?

The dusty road leads to the secluded cemetery, mostly shaded by large oaks, and surrounded by a chain link fence. It's one of the oldest cemeteries in the state, with at least one early birth date of 1808. It's deathly still around here. Appropriate.

Deep Creek Cemetery

People have reported a glowing tombstone in this cemetery. We won't stay late enough to see for ourselves because after we part company, I'm on my way to another glowing stone near Springtown. I'll tell you about that one.

Deep Creek Bridge is a short distance from the wondrous old gravestones. First, we leave here and walk up the hill we just walked down. Down is better.

Whispering bridge

We'll drive north to where the bridge should be. It is said that many years ago some children fell off into the creek, perhaps thirty feet or more. The date and the number of children are unknown. Reportedly, they were buried in Deep Creek Cemetery. I have found no proof, but then neither is there proof for many legends.

Yes, the bridge is just at the curve. Virginiae and I are getting out of the car and walking to the center. If you're afraid of heights, don't look down.

The story is, you can hear cries of the children who died in the creek.

Listen, do you hear?...I didn't hear crying and my friend Virginiae didn't either; however, there was an eerie moaning coming from the depths. It *could* be moaning of ghost-children.

Or it could be the wind.

Aurora

Green is a good color, but a little green man?

Now that we have heard the whispers of "Whispering Bridge," we are driving back toward 114 and Aurora Cemetery. The settlement of Aurora got its start in the 1850s, on an impressive terrain of oak and mesquite trees. That depends on how much one is impressed with mesquite trees, but they were here before the inhabitants.

The town grew rapidly for a time. In thirty years, population spiraled to over 2,000. Then tragedy struck. With an epidemic of what settlers called "spotted fever," and the railroad headed for nearby Rhome, residents moved away, leaving only a scattered few.

Then in 1897 someone had the grand idea of spreading the story about an airship landing in Aurora. Reportedly, a little green man crashed the ship into a windmill, smashing the structure and the craft into many pieces.

The green alien was also gone with the windmill. Since he didn't survive, a couple of citizens buried him in Aurora Cemetery but were reluctant to say where. This all came at a time when sightings of mysterious aircraft surfaced all over Texas—yes, way back then.

However, the story was eventually labeled a hoax, having been planned to bring interest back into the waning community. That tale of the airship just didn't fly.

However, bits of a "peculiar" alloy *were* found. Reportedly, as late as the 1960s, the McDonnell Aircraft Company analyzed it—not coming to a strong conclusion, other than agreeing it was an elaborate hoax. Few if any residents of Aurora still wonder if the story was true.

The above little bit of history sets the stage for a ghostly presence in the town, and takes up time while we are driving. Now that we have reached 114, we're back in the active community looking for the street sign, "Cemetery Road." It should be just ahead, still on the east side of town.

Okay, we've found the sign and are going south. The cemetery is about three miles down the road, which includes a curve to the left. This area is large and still in use. Veterans of the Civil War, both World Wars, and Korea and Vietnam Conflicts are buried here. As for the "alien" who piloted the aircraft of 1897, his remains were never exhumed. The idea had come up, but town fathers vetoed the proposal. Had they found the exact location, who would they have discovered in the grave? Jesse James?

Is a little green alien buried here?

It is said that strange anomalies can be seen after dark in this graveyard. Is it the apparition of the little green alien or other ghostly forms?

The cemetery is fenced, with a Historical Marker of the State of Texas mounted at one of the entrances. It mentions the alien spaceship crash as well as the 1891 "spotted fever" epidemic. The disease is currently referred to as a form of meningitis. Hundreds of citizens died and were buried in Aurora Cemetery. Since so many people died before their expected time, their spirits may still be restless, even after a hundred years.

Its main gate stands at the pedestrian entrance, flanked with two stone pillars. You don't have to be inside the grounds for a possible sighting of unnatural apparitions. On a still night, concentrate on luminous movements between the gravestones and high in the trees.

Aurora's borealis, or little green men looking for a lost comrade?

An Endangered Ghost

This tale comes from a friend to whom an elderly acquaintance related an experience of over half-a-century ago. It was not an experience the ninety-six-year-old gentleman, whom I'll call Mr. Hamilton, would likely forget.

The place is near Chico, just north of Bridgeport in northwestern Wise County. The settlement began in the mid-1870s when a Californian arrived and set up a general store near Dry Creek. First thing the limited number of residents knew, a community was born.

Later on, the town called itself the oil capital of the county. It was also known as a leading producer of crushed stone for road construction. Not that crushed stone has anything to do with the ghost of this story. The business wasn't formed until long after the ghost made her first appearance. Still, the stones were there, and slingshots have been around a long time.

According to my friend, Bob Hopkins, Mr. Hamilton and three other men had been buying cattle in West Texas. They grew tired during their long drive home to Chico.

At this time the road from Jacksboro cut through Wizard Wells. They had reached the old bridge that crossed the west fork of the Trinity. Keep in mind this was in 1949. The same place is now the north end of Lake Bridgeport.

The bridge—before the water became a lake

They pulled off the road, not that any abundance of traffic made it necessary, for they had seen few cars that afternoon. Getting out of the car to stretch their legs, one of the men heard splashing from the river. Figuring someone had chosen that particular spot to fish and was pulling a prize from the water, he strolled across the road.

The splashing became stronger. A woman's screams followed. Mr. Hamilton and his three friends rushed to the river's bank. Had it not been that they all witnessed the same thing, no one would have believed what they saw.

Moving toward them, just above the water, a woman's misty form thrashed about as if she were drowning. She continued down the river, rose over the bridge and down again onto the water. The horrified men ran after the ghostly shape and watched her disappear on the east bank, close to the site of Green Elm Cemetery.

Green Elm may have been easier for the ghost to find

The cemetery needs attention. Incidentally, the old steel bridge is still there, but impassable. The first gravestone appears to be from the early 1870s and the latest from the first decade of the twentieth century. There are around fifty gravesites, not all marked.

To reach the cemetery from Chico, head west toward Jacksboro on FM 1810. A few miles out of Chico (Robert L. Ripley said a few was eight), at the Jack County line, notice the sign, "Green Elm Cemetery." The dirt road can be muddy, so choose a nice sunny day. Follow the signs for four or five miles. The dirt almost runs out of road or vice versa. An oil field compressor station is on your right. The old graveyard is about 500 yards on down, and what is left of the road dead-ends at the cemetery. Makes sense.

Take someone with you if you choose to visit Green Elm. It would be frightening to be alone if you witnessed a woman dripping with water, making her wet way back to a grave. Besides, who would believe you?

Mr. Hamilton and his friends were not the only spectators of such a phenomenon. Other sightings of the endangered ghost have been reported through the years.

Who could the ghostly woman be? Many legends are based on drownings, but usually, some reason for the tragedy is included in the telling. This time, the reason is left up to our imagination.

Baccus

Texas has always been considered hot in summer and even hotter in the twenty-first century, but Baccus Cemetery may give you a chill or two on a hot day. It certainly isn't a choice spot for an evening stroll.

Driving north from Dallas, take either Preston Road or Hwy. 75 and turn west on Legacy. The cemetery is just east of the Tollway on the right.

Courtesy of Chris Moseley

Silence permeates the grounds, even though it's in a busy area with large contemporary buildings across the street. A chain link fence surrounds the flat terrain, with so few trees that it seems to be set back in time, with the appearance of a country cemetery.

In the early 1840s the Republic of Texas included the community of Plano within its boundaries. Most of the early settlers migrated from Tennessee and Kentucky. It wasn't easy to form any kind of community with all the Indian raids. Today, the town is a growing suburb of Dallas.

William Foreman is given credit for Plano's existence chiefly because of his enterprising business acumen. He built a gristmill and sawmill, much in demand by the area's residents. Other businesses were added and before long, the small town came into being, with a mail service begun around 1850.

Since Mr. Foreman rejected his name being used for the new little community, "Plano" was chosen. Postal authorities agreed, since the Spanish word means *plain* in English and suited the flat region.

During the Civil War the town declined, but hope prevailed. After the war, families returned and picked up where they left off. Fire destroyed Plano in the 1870s, but determined citizens would not admit defeat and the town prospered. It took on steady growth. It also took on steady death.

Note the orbs in upper right corner
Courtesy of Chris Moseley

The cemetery originally had "Cook" as its name. In the seventies Rachel Cook, daughter of Henry Cook, married Joseph

Baccus; therefore, they changed the name to *Baccus*. It is still in use, and Daniel Cook's grave is the oldest in Plano, if not in Collin County. As wars went on, many veterans were buried there.

Now back to this hot/cold thing. We know the cemetery is over 150 years old. We know fire destroyed the town at one time. What we don't know is what energy is forming the cold spots that seem to inject themselves into your arm or on your face.

Other anomalies have been reported late at night in Baccus Cemetery. Now you see them, now you don't. It is said you can feel a presence coming up behind you. Turn, and no one is there. Nonetheless, you can feel a chill in the Plano cemetery. That's the plain-o truth.

The Fort That Never Was

It was Christmas morning in the late 1880s in Montague County. Smoke plumes arose from the houses in the small settlement of Spanish Fort. A smell of gunpowder filled the air and three men lay dead—before breakfast. We don't know what time that was, but breakfast time doesn't change things. Dead is dead. Or is it?

Soon after the 1750s, the Taovayas Indians established villages on opposite sides of the river at what is now called Spanish Fort. History tells us the Spanish attacked the Taovayas, and after a battle of several hours, the Spanish retreated. They hadn't expected to face six thousand Indians.

Eventually, the two forces made peace with each other. After the Louisiana Purchase and a series of smallpox epidemics, the Taovayas left their collapsing villages.

Once Anglo-American settlers arrived upon the ruins, they assumed the Spaniards had deserted the site. Thus, the obvious name: Spanish Fort. It had never been a fort at all.

Spanish Fort served as a stopping place for drovers on their way up the Chisholm Trail. The settlement had a post office, doctors, hotels, and churches. Don't forget the saloons—all the makings of a thriving community. The place tried to survive, but it eventually became unmade.

Outlaws crossed the river to buy provisions in the settlement, nearly always causing some kind of ruckus with a gunshot or several. How many people did the citizens bury in the Old Spanish Fort Graveyard? Some graves had markers, many did not.

The trails moved westward. One citizen, Mr. Justin, even walked his boots right over to Nocona, where his boot company thrived for decades.

The "Old" cemetery is east of Farm Road 103, around fifteen miles north of Nocona. You might need a map for this one, but you can take 35 north to Gainesville and west on U.S. 82 to Nocona. No matter which direction you come from to Nocona, you still turn north on 103 to Spanish Fort.

You can see the old school and remains of deserted businesses and what used to be a real town square. It fits the mold of a ghost town.

If you make this trip at night, be prepared to drive past the new cemetery to the old one. It's a little tricky to find in the dark. Once you are finding your way with a flashlight, it may go out even if you had just inserted fresh batteries. When you return to the car, the flashlight will undoubtedly be good as new. Flashlights and recorders are known to become inactive in cemeteries. Electromagnetic energy in a graveyard sometimes does that.

It is said you will feel cold spots as you walk about the gravestones—not a freezing sensation, but a sharp coldness. Anyone who has ever been to Spanish Fort Cemetery can verify seeing movements through the trees. By the time you blink, thinking you may have been mistaken, nothing will be there. But the form may just as suddenly appear somewhere else.

Spirits of the many smallpox victims or cowboys and drovers who were murdered could be objecting to their early deaths and may want to tell you about them. Listen if you don't wish to appear superior. After all, you're a guest visiting their domain.

As in many country cemeteries, strange sounds come from the distance, or they may appear distant. One evening while visiting a country cemetery in Van Zandt County, I heard the most eerie sounds. They seemed to echo. A friend who accompanied me felt certain they were cows bellowing from the next farm. But it was way past their bedtime.

Don't be surprised if you hear sounds at Spanish Fort Cemetery. And another thing... you many feel, as others have, someone watching you. Don't expect it to be the sheriff of Montague County.

Play It Again

Being buried in two places seems to require an explanation. My friend Peggye Swenson told me about a man named J.E. Arrington and how he happened to be buried in two separate graves. Mr. Arrington's final resting places are in Friendship Cemetery, near Tolar, a few miles west of Granbury in Hood County. A road sign will direct you to the turn from Highway 377.

According to county records, J.E. was in his seventies when he lost his arm in 1897. Anyone with such an injury in those years was lucky to survive even for a short while. Mr. Arrington's family believed the only logical procedure was to bury the limb. It has a private site in the cemetery, complete with headstone, or perhaps that's armstone: "The arm, J.E. Arrington, amputated 1897."

Unfortunately, J.E. passed on a couple months later, but there wasn't room next to his appendage. He had to be buried more than an arm's length away.

At one time, the small area was overgrown with weeds but is now enclosed with a chain-link fence and is well kept. That means

J.E. Arrington's armstone

J.E. Arrington's tombstone

weeds seem to be mowed, even if no grass grows. In the spring, iris and wild flowers spread their beauty.

Several children's graves are marked with rocks or fieldstones. Any dates or names carved into them have long disappeared since fieldstone tends to wear away. The first legible date in this cemetery is 1880.

Mr. Arrington's story in itself is not a ghostly one, but a tragedy. It's the association the cemetery had with a small school next to it that provides the rest of the tale. The locals tell that the structure served as a school during the week and as a church on Sundays.

Peggye added that in her younger days, the kids used to "hang out" near the graveyard. You know, a quiet place where no one would bother them—or so they thought.

The community had moved away and the little church fell to ruin, held up by a few two-by-fours. Only an old upright piano, minus many keys, stood near the altar area under its deteriorating roof. Still, they may have been able to play Chopin's "Black-Key Etude" if only the white keys were missing. The young people used to plunk on the piano and dance on the rickety floor.

When it was dark, it was very very dark—the better to scare you with. One evening Peggye and her date, with another couple, drove up the winding dirt road to the cemetery. Their laughing ceased when sounds from a piano drifted in their direction.

They didn't know who else had planned to meet them, but they were anxious to see. As they drove closer, it became apparent no other car was present. Still hearing the melody, they stopped and hurried to the school in the wooded area.

The music abruptly ceased, but they saw no one. This ended their festivities for the evening. I don't know if it was "ladies first" or not, but they beat a retreat and jumped into the car, leaving in a whirl of dust.

They weren't the only ones who heard the piano and saw no one. Others who had heard the tales wanted to find out for themselves and had the same experience. Each episode was frightening and unexplainable. After an adult went to check it out, the young people were no longer harassed for making up a story.

The piano is gone and the area is now cleared away, with nothing left but a memory—and the cemetery of course.

When I first told this tale to someone, he replied, "Now I guess you're going to say Mr. Arrington's arm was playing the piano."

I did not say that.

A Stone's Glow Away

Picture yourself standing in a cemetery during a dark night. You are alone, of course, but are you? A bright glow appears through the trees. Now you wonder why you ventured by yourself to this country cemetery.

The story of this gravestone in Veal Station has been on the Texas news and in area newspapers. Someone had even reported a ghost-woman walking around the grounds. Rumors have to begin someplace.

Veal Station Cemetery

Thinking I would never locate the cemetery at night, I decided to find it first in the daytime. I obtained explicit instructions to drive to the fork in the road and turn right. Take notice of forks in the road. In this case, turn right *before* the fork, which is a hard turn to know.

That's how I got lost the first time. I made so many country turns, I found myself back in La Junta. Nothing wrong with that. La Junta is the town with all the wonderful garden statuary—but this trip I was looking for funerary statuary.

It was early so I stopped for a soda, just to kill time. I hope killing time won't make me a bad person. The thing is, the gravestone doesn't glow until dark. That's what I'd heard. I hadn't seen it yet.

While sipping my soda, I reviewed a little history of the place. The first white settlers founded Veal Station 150 years ago on horseback, and I had trouble finding it with directions. But it wasn't there before they founded it. That's the difference.

Originally, they referred to the location as Cream Hill, before naming it after an early settler, William G. Veal. The citizens placed a huge bell on top of one of the first buildings. They rang it when an attack by Indians was imminent.

A person could take the stagecoach for a dollar any day of the week to Weatherford. But even with the stage line, people were hesitant to flock to the community because of the Indian threat. Had they known a gravestone was forthglowing, their hesitancy might have been sealed.

By the mid-1880s Veal Station had become a farming center. Ten years later it boasted Parsons College with an estimated enrollment of 500 students coming from much of West Texas. Then the railroads...When the rails bypassed Veal Station, everything declined and all but a few residents moved away.

Having said that, it was time to meet my friends whom I will refer to as Jim and Laura. They had visited the cemetery before and promised to accompany me.

I asked Jim if he had ever heard the rumor of a ghostly woman. He replied, "I've never seen or heard of that one."

It sounds as if someone's imagination ran away. If there really was such an apparition, and I was afraid of the dark, I don't think she would be the one I'd turn to. Would she give me a consoling pat on the shoulder, or *through* my shoulder?

Dusk finally turned into dark. The entrance was on the south side of the road, and the gate was securely padlocked—as always after dusk. I had heard the area was citizen-patrolled to guard against outsiders. And an "insider" in a cemetery would be...?

We parked the car facing west, close to the fence and east of the big gate. Laura said that at just the right angle we could see the glowing stone from the car. That might not be a bad idea—not leaving the car I mean.

However, the foliage was thick and I think one tree limb blocked my view. We got out and walked through the pedestrian gate.

Jim said, "I've been over here several times, and I've seen that stone glow on cloudy, cloudless, as well as rainy nights."

This night was clear, with a slip of a quarter-moon, and I did not need an umbrella. It hadn't rained in months. Not a cricket chirped as we walked a little further into the cemetery.

So far I hadn't located the stone. I asked Jim if he could see it. He didn't have to answer. As if on cue, a bright glow appeared in the depths of the cemetery.

The glowing stone

"There!" I said, "I see it. That glow isn't coming from a *Rolling Stones* glow-in-the-dark T-shirt!"

The stone didn't shine forth like a beacon on a lighthouse. It appeared solid, a little bluish-white with uneven edges.

It was not a reflection from the moon or any light poles. An old-timer who lived close by vowed he had seen the glowing gravestone long before electricity was in the area.

I can only attest to the fact it was spooky.

In Veal Station Cemetery, there are other stones nearly identical in style, color, and age. Only one gravestone glows. If a phenomenon cannot be explained scientifically, then something eerie is going on.

The stone seemed to draw us forward while at the same time warning us to stay back. The glow disappeared. We had gotten too close. I believed my eyes then believed it was time to go home.

I walked backwards, which wasn't easy under the circumstances. Within a few yards, the stone again served as its own spotlight—bright as ever.

We climbed into the car and decided to stop for coffee.

That was fine with me. We had time to kill.

Light is a form of energy, and to be created, an energy source must be supplied. The question is "What kind of energy?"

Incandescence is light from heat energy.

Luminescence is cold light.

According to the Fluorescent Mineral Society, "There are several varieties of luminescence, each named according to what the source of energy is."

Ghostly light? Reflect on that.

The Drowned Woman

Almost without fail, people on a wagon train knew where to find watering holes or ponds before they ever left on a journey. They learned it from those who had traveled before them and had made a map. Copies of maps were often available in livery stables so travelers could have access to them before ever leaving home. Occasionally a wooden sign would be stuck in the ground along the trail, with an arrow and "water" carved on it.

As a rule, someone may have tested the water to see if it was fit to drink. But this story would have made them think twice about whether or not anyone would want to be an official taster.

In 1854 the Texas legislature provided a Comanche Reservation on the Clear Fork of the Brazos, where good water and hunting prevailed. The Comanches cultivated crops, but extreme drought kept them from producing all they needed. In 1859 the government removed the Comanches to Indian Territory.

That information determines the approximate date the following tragedy might have occurred. That is, providing Comanches were responsible. If not, white men could have murdered the woman and you can disregard the part about the Comanches. But it *is* a little bit of history worth remembering, and the story still has its beginning in the 1800s.

The infamous watering hole involved is fifteen miles south of Stephenville on Highway 281, on a slight rise just outside of Clairette in Erath County. It is now on private property.

As the story goes, either white men or Indian raiders abducted a white woman from a wagon train. They took her away, beat and assaulted her, then left her for dead. But she didn't die. She struggled to her feet and followed tracks to a watering hole.

Other travelers were at the water-stop when she limped up, screaming about the attackers. She was near hysteria, and her accusations were not taken seriously.

One of the women prepared a place by the fire for her to spend the night. Exhausted, she finally drifted off to sleep. When everyone awakened the following morning, the woman was gone.

The travelers assumed she had regained her senses and left the camp for home. Their alternative speculation was perhaps some of the men she accused earlier at the watering hole actually had attacked her and returned to silence her.

A few days later her body surfaced from the pond. She was buried nearby beneath the branches of an oak tree.

It didn't take long for the story about the woman to get around. As a matter of fact, people wanted to see the watering hole more because of the stories they had heard than for water.

However, travelers who stopped to camp by the pond often ran into a woman dressed in wet clothing, with bruises on her face, and looking as if she had been pulled from the water. Only at night did she venture to all who camped there. She looked into their eyes, wondering if they were responsible for her death. "Were you the ones?" she asked.

If anyone tried to talk to her, she wouldn't answer. After gazing at each of them, she turned and walked back into the water, disappearing. This left the travelers stunned and immeasurably frightened. For quite a while, no one went near the pond.

When enough time lapsed, allowing the story to die down, strangers once again stopped at the watering hole. Sometimes the woman appeared and sometimes not. But those who did see her when she looked closely at their faces could never recall what she looked like. They saw her, but yet they didn't.

How can she be in a watery grave when she was buried under the tree with a flat stone marking the site?

Is her spirit rising from the water, not allowing her to find eternal rest until she recognizes her attackers?

Do you agree if the men—whether white or Indian—ever returned to the watering hole, the woman's spirit would cause them to die of fright?

It's the Spirit

The German word "poltergeist" is commonly translated as "noisy ghost." That does not mean you can carry on a conversation even if you speak German fluently. As a matter of fact, after a poltergeist has had her fun, there is no one left to converse with.

"Her" is used since poltergeists are reportedly girls more than boys. Research by paranormal experts shows this is true. Whether or not the girl poltergeists are venting their frustrations for whatever reason has not fully been determined.

According to some studies, while poltergeist activity is surely paranormal, it has nothing to do with spirits. Still, this tale seems to incorporate both.

An acquaintance of mine who lives in North Texas has related this story to me with the promise I wouldn't divulge her name or the location of her house. However, capturing the spirit of this book in progress, she agreed to tell of her family's experiences. Capturing the spirit in their home is something else entirely.

We can understand why the value of the young couple's property might take a downward trend. Never have I seen a classified ad requesting a home occupied by spirits, unless of course, they wanted it equipped with a wine cellar.

I will call my friend Alicia. When they first moved into their house, they hadn't noticed the small graveyard on their property. Wild vines twined amongst the trees and covered the old gravestones. At a later time they decided to clear the debris so the sites could have the respect they deserved. In summer, after the area had been cleared, wild crocus appeared as if they had been dormant for many years.

Alicia noticed one of the graves was that of a child, obviously the daughter of other family members buried there. This saddened her since she and her husband were parents of a lovely ten-year-old daughter, Elizabeth. Alicia understood the feelings the dead child's mother and father must have had when their little one died. On Christmas, she and her daughter placed flowers on the child's grave.

According to author Troy Taylor, cemeteries may possibly be "doorways" leading from one world to another. As many American Indians have done in the past, they chose an area for their burial grounds they believed to be sacred in the first place. Perhaps our own ancestors chose such sacred burial sites by being unconsciously drawn to them.

One evening Alicia was reading after her family had gone to bed. She heard a familiar sound.

"Mama?" The sound was that of a little girl's voice.

It startled Alicia since she knew Elizabeth had to be asleep. She got up from her chair and walked toward the hallway.

"Mama, can you help me?"

Alicia hurried up the stairs to her daughter's bedroom. "Elizabeth, what's wrong?" Her child was sound asleep. Thinking it was only a bad dream, she turned and went back downstairs to finish her book and turn off the lights.

This episode was the first time Alicia had heard the voice, and she saw no reason to mention it, still thinking her daughter had been dreaming. A few nights later when she and her husband, Jim, were downstairs watching television, she heard the same call. The parents rushed up to Elizabeth's room. This time Alicia awoke her daughter and asked if she had a bad dream. She did not remember dreaming and soon drifted back to sleep.

From then on, both Alicia and Jim were very much attentive to anything out of the ordinary. Several weeks passed when one morning Alicia found the throw she had left on her chair the night before, lying on the floor. Also, during the night, her husband went to check on clinking sounds coming from the kitchen but found nothing.

Another time Elizabeth's favorite doll she always took to bed with her was on the ottoman in front of the fireplace. The previous night Alicia had pulled the covers up around the doll at the same time she said goodnight to Elizabeth.

Several weeks passed without disturbances of any kind, except for the clear sound of "Mama, will you come?" Alicia always went to check on her daughter, even though she knew she would be asleep. She could only surmise the actions and voice were those of the little girl from the small graveyard. Just in case, she still visited her grave and reassured the child that everything would be all right.

If it *was* the child's spirit, it did no harm. If anything, she helped bring a mother's love that much closer to her own daughter.

At first Alicia and Jim were very concerned and even considered moving as soon as possible. As time passed, they almost looked forward to their little visitor. Of course, when they *do* decide to move, they don't know what prospective buyers might think if they tell them.

For now they believe that keeping the right spirit can do wonders.

ffiinter's Chapel

With land being purchased in the 1960s for the Dallas/Fort Worth Airport, many small cemeteries were either moved or otherwise affected. Several of them contained the graves of hundreds of Texas pioneers. Minter's Chapel was one of these cemeteries.

When reports first surfaced concerning paranormal activity in Minter's Chapel, at least one reason became feasible to those who knew the history of this cemetery.

Whose spirits would be so restless that they gave visitors the distinct impression they were being watched? It may be possible they wanted to know if more of their hallowed ground was going to become a runway.

Perhaps the following account offered one theory: Green W. Minter, born in 1803 in Virginia, married Jane Large in Tennessee and migrated to Texas in the mid-1840s. They first chose Dallas but a few years later moved to Tarrant County.

According to the 1979 writings of Bertie Cates, his granddaughter, her father gave the land for the first church. These God-fearing men cut the logs and built the chapel, which was used alternately for a school.

Citizens of Minter's Chapel could not have dreamed giant flying airships would one day take off and land at an International Airport, disturbing the community they had worked so hard to develop.

The cemetery is located on West Airfield Drive, a quarter of a mile north of the Glade Road intersection. Because the airport is on private property, expect security police to be patrolling the area should you venture there at night.

As one "ghoststalker" walked through the area thought to be haunted, a dash of cold struck him. The chill is said to be an essence of the physical manifestation of the spirit. The same visitor reported a strong sense of being watched. Assuming he didn't mean being watched by a wild rabbit or the police, could the spirits of those who had been disturbed with the construction of the airport still be keeping watch by night? It presents an interesting theory.

We know to be respectful in cemeteries. This is one cemetery in which you would do well to speak gently to whomever or whatever else might be patrolling—in and out the gravestones. You would not want your flight to be canceled.

St. Olaf's Kirche

Ever hear voices and there's no one there? And if anyone is walking on air, it may be ghosts. That in itself is unnerving, but not knowing the source is downright eerie.

Cranfils Gap is forty-two miles northwest of Waco on highway 6 at the junction of County Road 219 in Bosque County.

It's easy to see how it got its name. First, George Eaton Cranfil settled in the area in 1851. Second, it's near a gap in a mountain.

By 1890 the little town had about three stores and the mandatory saloon where many a cowboy hung his hat. Or maybe he just tipped it back on his head while imbibing a shot of whiskey and playing out a poker hand. The town boasted a livery stable, a blacksmith, and at least one church, a few miles away.

Cleng Peerson was credited for bringing Norwegian immigrants to Texas. They first settled in Norse and built St. Olaf's near Cranfils Gap in 1886. By 1917 the citizens began moving closer to town and built a new brick ediface there, no longer wanting to drive to the church in the country.

However it is the old church and its adjacent cemetery that are responsible for this tale. The tombstones are dated from the early- to mid-1800s.

If ever "Here's the church and here's the steeple" fit a structure, the label goes on this rock edifice plastered in white, with its bell tower reaching heavenward. The chandeliers, or perhaps they should be called suspended light fixtures, never had electricity. In the 1800s they could have used candles and later gaslights.

I can picture the services, especially at Christmas. A large wood stove heated the church. It must have touched the senses with its crackling logs and smell of cedar-bough decorations.

The story goes that if you enter the church, be sure it's for the right reason, such as to worship, or to take yourself back a century or more, for nostalgia's sake. If you try to entice Norwegian voices to speak or sing, music seems to accomplish it. Enticing the voices would be the wrong reason. Also, no specific melody is necessary.

St. Olaf's Kirche and Cemetery

The voices have been heard, not in a soothing way, but angry. That being the case, I believe "The 23rd Psalm" is a good choice.

Some people believe voices rise from the old cemetery outside the church. Where else? But the windows are closed. Perhaps the spirits could be inside the church. Many Norwegians were buried in the graveyard, so perhaps the voices belong to their spirits.

It is well known the faithful may return in spirit form to the church in which they once worshiped. They could be looking for salvation they have not yet found.

Ed Syers wrote about St. Olaf's in his book *Ghost Stories of Texas.* Mark Angle and his father, Lee, of Lee Angle's Photography Inc. in Fort Worth, accompanied Mr. Syers to this church in the late 1970s. The Angles' primary reason for going was to photograph the church's architecture for a historical film Lee Angle was preparing.

In the year 2001 Mark recalls his experience of the earlier time. His father had taken some pictures then climbed the stairs with Ed Syers to the little balcony.

Since a piano stood by the altar, Mark couldn't resist sitting down to play. At the time, his repertoire consisted of "Clair de Lune" and "Greensleeves." He chose the former as being more appropriate.

From behind him, voices began to mumble. The men weren't sure if the voices were speaking or singing. Mark couldn't hear them as he played, but his father could hear the voices coming from the back of the sanctuary.

Mr. Angle then took his son's place at the piano, thinking the voices were speaking in answer to the instrumental accompaniment. Mark ventured to the balcony and also clearly heard the voices, but neither man could pinpoint their origin.

Mark, however, said that although they couldn't make out the words, he remembers the sounds as being sweet more than angry, as has been earlier reported. I rather like that interpretation.

I have spoken with a young woman who has been to St. Olaf's Church on more than one occasion. Her name is Cindi. She said the second time she visited the desolate area, the church still sent chills right through her. No, she didn't call it quaint. Perhaps if the ghostly tales had never been reported, the little church with its tall bell tower would have indeed been described as quaint.

Cindi said when she and three friends arrived, the day was still, but the gates rattled at the cemetery entrance. That tempted her to leave, but they continued inside. She observed shadows of people walking through the sanctuary, very aware of more shadows than people.

Another comment I have heard from more than one source is that a caretaker guards St. Olaf's. He is apparently opposed to those who come to disturb the spirits resting within the church's rattling gates.

When you drive up the dirt road, the church appears on your left. "Appears" seems to fit because the church sits alone on top of a hill—stark, but ethereal. The little church is still used on special occasions, and weddings are frequently held there.

The afternoon we visited St. Olaf's, I had planned to sing "The Lord's Prayer" and let you know if I heard mumbling voices. However, workmen were there at the same time, repairing the

Saint Olaf Cemetery

church's roof. I was afraid the roofers might have thought I was a bit weird, so I didn't burst into song. Besides, the voices might have really been confused. Mark Angle's verification was good enough for me.

Step Softly

Jn the still of the night, you can hear them crying.

Stroll over a narrow wooden bridge covering meandering Ish Creek, and you will come to an old cemetery. The creek bed is dried out from lack of rain. Perhaps in 1903 it flowed with cool clear water when the Berachah Home first existed on twenty-seven acres of Tarrant County land.

The Reverend J.T. Upchurch founded Berachah, a Home for Unwed Mothers. The name was taken from a scripture in Chronicles II—"Valley of Blessings." Some of the young women were runaways. Often, parents sent their daughters there to have their babies, and other girls were homeless. Once they found themselves pregnant, in most cases, they found themselves homeless. In the early days, families often banished their "betrayed" daughters.

Some of the mothers-to-be did not arrive until later on in their pregnancies. They did not always have proper medical care, causing a pregnancy and delivery to be risky. It soon

Berachah Rescue
Society Historical
Marker

became necessary to provide a cemetery on the property.

Dallas and Fort Worth businessmen helped fund the Home, and eventually it expanded to more than forty acres. In 1921, as the institution progressed, it had seven separate structures. One, the girls' dormitory, was a three-story house with a screened-in porch. The Home also included a separate building for the nursery, in which as many as thirty-five babies were cared for at one time. A large maternity hospital occupied another structure.

The additional four buildings housed the contagious disease infirmary, the gardener's quarters, a printing shop, and laundry. In the industrial building the girls made handkerchiefs they sold. They also had a chapel and attended daily classes, including Bible study.

Later an auditorium seating 1,000 people was added. They used it for concerts, various programs, and probably religious meetings.

Dallas' E.M. Dealy's article in the January 1921 issue of *The Purity Crusader* describes the Home. "So far as is known, the Berachah Home is the only organization of its kind in the nation in which the young mothers are allowed to keep and rear their children...The young women are themselves trained during the day in a proper knowledge of grammar school subjects, in stenography, in art, in music, in nursing, in domestic science, in printing and in Bible study.

"During its first seventeen years of existence, over 1,100 persons, including girls and children, have been admitted and records show that about seventy-five percent of these girls have been restored to honorable and useful lives."

It was estimated that for lack of room, the Home found it necessary to reject an average of ten girls a month. The Home also hesitated to accept girls who had "sunk" to using morphine, even though they pleaded to stay just until their babies were born. The staff wanted to keep the young women who had only one major mishap in their lives separated from those who had apparently made many mistakes.

Girls or their parents sent applications from all over the state as well as throughout the country. The Home was that well thought of.

Many babies were stillborn or died soon after birth. Often the young mothers also died. While the cemetery was the final resting place of others associated with the Home, most of the graves held the babies.

If the mother did not name her child, its stone merely read "Baby No. 1," followed by the next grave with a number of an unnamed baby or toddler. Several had only first names engraved on their stones, all in a neat row.

Infant No. 14

Many years ago, around a hundred gravesites were visible. Now with grasses growing over the flat stones, only a few aboveground can be seen. The cemetery is contained within a chain-link fence on land owned by the University of Texas at Arlington.

The Home was sold in 1935 because of the Reverend Upchurch's health and the established Edna Gladney Home in Fort Worth. The land is now a park. All that is left of the Berachah Home for Unwed Mothers is a cemetery.

During my visit there I was intrigued to see a small child's pink and white cloth candy bag, the old-fashioned kind little ones used to carry homemade candies in. It rested on one of the small graves. The day was still, or wind might have blown it away. I supposed a little visitor had dropped it there. Someone could have left it on purpose as a remembrance, or could it be more mystical than that?

It is said if you wander out among the wooded park and into the cemetery late in the evening, you can hear babies crying.

...Step softly. Dreams rest here.

Diggin' Up Bones

John B. is where? John Bunyan Denton was killed during the battle of Village Creek in 1841. It is how he died and what happened to his bones that form the basis for this tale. There could be more than one reason for his restlessness.

The battle took place in eastern Tarrant County, along the banks of Village Creek, a tributary of the Trinity River. Tonkawas, Caddo, and Cherokees lived in their villages along the banks of the river. Naturally, friction existed between the Indians and settlers coming in from the east. The government of the Republic of Texas tried punitive attacks against the Indians in order to protect the settlers.

The villages may as well have had electronic security gates. These expeditions of 1838 failed to find the Indians' exact locations. The attacks, did, however, annoy the Indians, and they increased their own raids against the frontier settlements.

Three years later General Edward H. Tarrant organized volunteers from the Red River counties. They discovered one of the smaller villages and took its occupants by surprise.

Captain Denton did not have it so easy. He led his unit along the creek of the Trinity in attack against the Keechi village. The Indians had been alerted and gave strong opposition.

The history of the battle of Village Creek tells us Indian musketry killed Denton and wounded very few other militiamen. Denton was the only fatality.

According to *The Handbook of Texas*, Denton's men brought his body back and buried him in a "unmarked grave on the east bank of Oliver Creek, near its confluence with a stream now called Denton Creek."

The legend is that John's soul still haunts the area where he was buried on the prairie.

One of the reported seven men who helped bury Captain Denton was Henry Stout of Wood County. According to Stout, thirty-eight years after the burial, Major Jarvis of Fort Worth called upon him to look for the captain's gravesite and return his bones to Denton County.

A reporter interviewed Henry Stout for *"The Weekly Gazette, Fort Worth, Texas, Friday, July 1, 1887."*

In his account, "Death of John B. Denton," Mr. Stout said that after Denton was shot, he and the other men chose a place beneath a tree to bury the captain. When Major Jarvis asked Stout to set out on this mission, he furnished the man with a horse and Stout headed out to a strip of land he hadn't seen in decades. The ex-soldier commented that Peter Smith went along with him on the search.

Even though the country had changed some, by the time they got to the general area, he could tell by the terrain that he was on the right trail—"up the forks of Fossil and Trinity and around near Birdville."

When they approached a Mr. Pulliam working in the cornfield, the farmer asked the two men if they were looking for Denton's grave. Stout said he was one of seven men who buried him. The man laughed, replying that so far 500 men had claimed to have buried Denton.

At last Stout found a certain leaning tree he recognized as the one under which they had laid the captain to rest. Although the grave was unmarked, he knew right where to commence diggin' up bones. They knew they belonged to Denton.

But wait. Another account has been written about John's bones. John W. Gober stated to the *Denton News* that Denton's remains were buried on the "Waide Place." Also, Colonel Chisum had helped bury him. He knew the bones were Denton's because of the skeletal broken arm and the condition of his teeth. No doubt about it. Chisum reburied Denton in a wooden box in his yard on Clear Creek, near Bolivar.

Now you might wonder, would the ghost of John Denton roam the spot where he was originally buried or would his spirit go along with his bones to his final resting place?

That is why this author, for the present, is a storyteller and not a paranormalist. I can only speculate. We reason that when a person is killed violently or his life on earth is ended before he has finished what he considers his mission in this world, he refuses to pass over into the *next* world.

In Henry Stout's earlier statement, he said that if John B. had not thought the ground too boggy and had crossed anyway, he would not have been killed. Perhaps John's ghost wants to keep trying until he gets it right. Or he may be looking for his men and wants to return to his company. Whatever the reason, Captain Denton's ghost has been reported with earnest beliefs.

In 1901 the Pioneer Association of Denton County again removed his remains and buried them in the "southeast corner of the Denton County Courthouse lawn."

Captain Denton led an interesting and motivated life. He had been orphaned at the age of twelve. He left his adoptive home in Tennessee at an early age, studied law, preaching, and farming. According to Henry, John was considered a good and pious man, and "a more daring spirit never lived."

Or died? May Captain Denton rest in peace, no matter how many graves his bones have occupied.

Ghost Mountain

Mountains in North Texas? What used to be a rural community is now a thriving suburb of Dallas. Cedar Hill was founded in the 1850s, with a deadly tornado striking that same decade. No one has said the tornado brought with it an eerie graveyard, although it could have stirred things up a bit.

A branch of the Chisholm Trail once passed through the area of Cedar Hill in the rolling terrain of southwestern Dallas County. Apparently something or someone else also passed through. Perhaps they stayed.

The graveyard is called Mt. Pleasant, also known as "Ghost Mountain." It is sometimes referred to as "Old Hill Cemetery" and "Witch Mountain," but the name above the gate is "Mt. Pleasant." The name doesn't change the mysterious atmosphere. Whatever it is called, it can still be haunted.

Directions first, then the tale. Driving down 67 toward Cedar Hill, take the Beltline exit and turn right, toward the towers. After driving over a large hill, you should see Lake Ridge Road. Turn left and look for Bluebonnet Street. This takes you to the cemetery—should you decide to accept this mission.

Urban legends often tell us early occult activities took place in very old graveyards. In Athens' catacombs, inverted pentagrams and other satanic signs were left behind in the underground cavern, perhaps for as long as a century. The reputation of Ghost Mountain has apparently turned into an urban legend.

Some of the stones date to the early 1800s. According to Chris Moseley, a Dallas parapsychologist, teenagers used to try time and again to locate the "goat man" or ghost they were certain could be seen in the cemetery after nightfall. Mt. Pleasant had been vandalized several times in those days.

More than one grave appeared as an open pit, as if exhumations had taken place, making this the kind of cemetery you could really get into. When a body was exhumed, it was most likely for relocation (no DNA testing then). If the body *was* moved, the excavation should have been filled. We can only speculate.

Unless you have the power of invisibility, don't try to enter the cemetery gate at night. Police patrol this residential area built next to the cemetery.

Remember the cemetery was there first. The neighborhood welcome wagon may roll around with a headless driver, right up to the doors of these new homes.

The cemetery has been cleaned more than once in recent years and is usually free of weeds. Headstones previously turned over have been straightened, with the hope that they are at the original gravesites.

One dusky early evening I visited Mt. Pleasant and experienced nothing unusual. That is, unless that translucent wispy . . . Let me put it this way. I drove to the cemetery merely to have a look at it, since I knew of its reputation for being haunted.

A distinct breeze had formed when I first got out of my car. As I approached the gate, everything became still, not a leaf fluttering. I was not expecting anything but an old graveyard, much like I've encountered during genealogical research. The feeling here was not one of fright, but an awareness of the unusual.

I tried to look as if I were hunting for great-grandfather Munro Fore's gravesite, in case the authorities wondered. (Of course, Munro is actually buried in Waco and I knew that.) At that moment, a mist formed somewhere among the lengthening shadows, giving the suggestion of a light sprinkle. I headed back to the car, glancing alternately toward gravestones on my right and those same lengthening shadows on my left.

It occurred to me if I turned around quickly, what could have been behind me would then be in plain sight. I planned to have my key in the ignition before I could say *arrivederci* to the spirits of Ghost Mountain.

I cannot say this cemetery is haunted. You might decide that for yourself, especially if you encounter more than a mist.

On my drive back to Fort Worth, I hummed the "Hall of the Mountain King," which somehow came to mind.

Return to Ghost Mountain

Cindy Ritcheson gives us reason to make a return trip to Ghost Mountain. Mt. Pleasant, the cemetery's official name, is secluded—you don't see it on your way to a mall.

Drive down a winding road, or perhaps you drive up the road since the cemetery is nestled on a bluff on the outskirts of Cedar Hill.

Cindy first visited this graveyard with her teenage friends, mainly to tell ghost stories. As far as she knew, the plot on which they chose to sit had no family connection. She was simply drawn to the lovely old gravestones.

This unusual tale begins several years later when she married Dane Ritcheson. Dane's great uncle mentioned his genealogy research as well as a surname found on Ghost Mountain. He asked the young couple to take photographs of the family markers.

The request seemed exciting and only a little bit eerie. They planned the visit for a sunny autumn afternoon so the photography session would have the best light. Cindy wondered if she could find her way around in the daytime, since years before she had always gone after dark.

A curious coincidence occurred when her husband's ancestors turned out to be buried in the same plot around which she and her friends had shared ghost stories when they were in high school.

Nothing had ever manifested itself during all the nighttime visits—not a single shiver. She assumed an afternoon would be devoid of anything strange. But "strange" can happen anytime.

When they drove into the cemetery, a broken gravestone lay in the gravel road. They thought of moving it but decided against it. They would leave that up to the caretaker.

Cameras in hand, they exited the car and managed to get through the only gate Cindy had ever used in the past. The metal fence was not in good shape, but then it hadn't been in decades.

They walked toward the south end of the old graveyard to the family plot that overlooked the piney woods. They found the perfect spot from which to take pictures. Just as Dane clicked the shutter they froze. They heard what seemed to be something being dragged, followed by a metallic thud.

Freshly turned earth on an old grave?
Courtesy of Cindy Ritcheson

They called "Hello!" but got no answer. Instead, a "chink, chink, chink" resounded, similar to metal on metal.

The woods at that end of the graveyard were overgrown, and Cindy thought a maintenance crew was merely thinning out overgrowth. Any calmness disappeared when they became aware someone or some*thing* was coming towards them. Crunching of fall leaves made that clear. The feeling of being watched, especially in a graveyard, can be unmistakable. Their sensation seemed a mirror image. With every step they took, the couple felt others were taking the same steps on the reverse side of the sweeping tree.

They finally realized the situation they were in, and fear became reality. The thought of impending danger sent them to their car. They walked backwards—not an easy task—to see who or what might follow.

They hurriedly drove down the road to Cedar Hill. Being suspicious, they called police, even though they had little to report. The dispatcher said they checked the cemetery every two hours and the last report showed no broken headstone in the road!

What could the mysterious noises be? Was someone stalking the Ritchesons?

Later the same day, after police investigated, the facts came to light. "Grave Robbers at Work!"

The officers searched the spot where the Ritchesons had been. They found a coffin in the woods. The would-be grave robbers had extracted it from the ground. The sound the couple had heard came from the dragging of the coffin. It can be speculated the "chinking" sound was from the culprits trying to pry open the casket. The suspects left the coffin unopened and had fled by the time the police arrived.

At the time, Satanic cults were rumored to hold meetings in the Cedar Hill woods. The police theorized they had planned to take the coffin with them. The "open pits" mentioned in the earlier tale of Ghost Mountain may have been the work of grave robbers.

Cindy looks back to her teenage years when she and her friends purposely *tried* to scare themselves on Ghost Mountain. But as an adult on a mild afternoon, she had a fright she would never forget.

Recently, she and her husband returned to Ghost Mountain to take more pictures. The posted warning against vandals would surely make an impression on anyone considering such an act.

Who knows, the ghosts of Ghost Mountain may have their own security police.

Migration

In the early 1850s the name White Settlement referred to a few isolated farms and a couple of trading posts west of Fort Worth. An organized community developed, remaining a frontier outpost until the threat of Indian attacks disappeared. A hundred years later, Carswell Air Force Base and General Dynamics, now Lockheed Martin, helped spur its growth.

In the 1950s the White Settlement Cemetery, also known as "Pecan Grove" and "Grant," was located east of Grants Lane and south of the north/south runway at the main entrance of what used to be called the Bomber Plant. A sign atop the original cemetery lych gate, read "White Settlement," with "1857" on a smaller gate next to it. A lych gate, or "corpse gate," served as the entrance for the wagon bearing the coffin and family members. Friends entered through the smaller one.

When a phenomenon occurs in a graveyard, the more people reporting it, the more credence is given to the story.

The informant of this ghostly tale remembers well when he attended a party one October night over forty years ago. He reportedly crashed the party and at the age of ten, was the youngest person there. Part of the planned activity was to visit White Settlement Cemetery and be scared. "It would be fun," the kids said.

As the boys reached the perimeter of the graveyard, they noticed a low mist forming on the ground. Mesmerized by the dry ice appearance of the mist, they continued walking until halfway through the large cemetery.

By this time the mist had risen until it resembled a field of ghostly apparitions. The younger boy, now a man in his fifties, said he would not forget the fright that engulfed him. He never returned to White Settlement Cemetery. Others have reported the same experience in their young lives.

In the early 1950s, as Convair grew, runways had to be extended. The only available ground for expansion contained 350 graves. Fort Worth's Oakwood Cemetery on Grand Avenue would be their final home.

After the coffins were removed, the runway was extended over the now available space.

The question is, did the spirits of White Settlement Cemetery linger at the location of the original burial? Or did they float alongside their earthly remains during their migration to Oakwood?

If mist continues to radiate upwards from old runways, it might be natural steam on concrete. Unless....

Skip-a-Rope

Laughing children and a jump rope...

In 1884 the community of Lingleville was known as Needmore but it was renamed in honor of John Lingle, who had been one of its first settlers ten years earlier. The small town is ten miles west of Stephenville on Highway 8 in Erath County. The land was dense with oak trees, a beautiful forestland. It is still picturesque.

A country school near Lingleville was built on a hill, or at least on an incline. It eventually turned to dust. Perhaps it did not literally do so, but with time, it died. The school's spirit may rest in School Hill Cemetery.

After the old school closed and deteriorated, the new one was built elsewhere. The previous location then became the site of School Hill Cemetery, an appropriate name. Reach it by turning northeast off Highway 8 onto 397. Don't mistake Lower School Hill Cemetery on the right, which is on private property. An aged church still stands in front of the cemetery.

This is a dirt road, and even though it is regularly graded, a dry day is advised for a visit.

Listen to the children

Apparitions of buffalo that once roamed the hills of Erath County do not rumble across the land as one might expect. However, something strange occurs when you visit the cemetery. Listen carefully while you are there. You will seldom hear road traffic, except from local residents. Listen for laughter—the sound of children playing in a schoolyard. That is the legend.

According to Dave Juliano of *The Shadowlands*, the theory is that former school sites may have a buildup of psychic energies of emotional events having previously transpired there. This is an open invitation to spirits.

The usual pattern of a school being constructed over an unknown cemetery was reversed. In this case, the story is that the cemetery overlapped the old foundation of the school. Still, some people who had been students in the little school on the hill lived and died in Lingleville. They were buried in this cemetery.

An individual who desires anonymity said he and his fiancée drove to School Hill to see if the tale of children playing were true. After waiting an hour or so, they decided to leave. The only movement had been the moon sliding from behind a cloud.

Then something incredible occurred. They witnessed the misty form of what appeared to be a little girl. It looked as if two other forms stood next to her. Just as the children began taking turns skipping rope, they stopped, floating away in a slow swirl. It was as if they knew someone had been watching.

The couple heard no laughter but vowed the apparitions were clear. They stared, knowing beyond a shadow of a shade, what they witnessed had indeed happened. They still did not believe it.

Would you?

Ronda's Grave

Was she a good witch or a bad witch? Which?

In a cemetery that is a little inconvenient to locate, a rock crypt once stood but is now mostly gone. It has been there so long, the latter was inevitable.

Is this Ronda's crypt?

The area near what used to be the community of Ronda is pure history. It developed in the early 1880s, and the first citizen to pass on became the first resident of Ronda Cemetery. The community was off to a good start with a post office, school, a store, and about seventy-five people. When a town loses its post office, it often begins to lose its population. This was Ronda's fate when in 1907, the post office moved to nearby Harrold. The school consolidated with theirs as well.

All that is left of the small community of Ronda is the cemetery—and Ronda's ghost. It is thought the town was named after her. The dates are no longer on her marker, so her birth year is not known.

Ronda Cemetery

The fact is, Ronda the person is said to have been a witch. Through the years people have reported seeing her apparition rise from the crypt, glide around the headstones for a time, then return to her resting place and disappear.

According to the meaning of given names, Ronda or Rhonda denotes a person of dignified nature, with an appreciation for the deeper aspects of life. That is, the aspects of life contained in religious theories and occult beliefs.

A "Ronda" requires time alone, especially in the outdoors, in order to cope with the pressures of life. And death?

Further research along this line states the name causes tension that affects respiratory organs, resulting in bronchial conditions. Having said that, the legend concerning Ronda's death says that she died of the flu.

Finding the cemetery without explicit directions may be about as easy as baking a Black Forest cake without a recipe. My sister is accompanying me as navigator on this trip.

Let's hear it for *Back Roads of Texas* maps. I'd hate to have a flat on a country road and be stranded...at night...in the dark.

From Electra, you can drive south on 25 to FM 1811, then turn left on FM 2326. Ronda Cemetery will be on the left, about ten miles from town.

Since we're driving from the south, we take 25, turn west at FM 2326, and follow the road to Ronda. We will pass by Beaver Creek Cemetery before the road takes its next right turn to our destination. We should zero in on it depending on how clever we are with that south/west thing.

I never expected it to be so desolate. Only a mesquite tree or two are on the land. Another tree couldn't find a vacant spot to grow. It is a country cemetery on open range, in desperate need of a clean-up crew. A blanket of cactus covers many graves, especially one that is surrounded by a strong iron fence.

Hmm, look at all the Spanish dagger plants, the ones that spray out, with pods hanging from the top. Sharp! Be careful... and the devil's claw. I haven't seen those since I was a youngster. Ronda is familiar with them all.

A cactus coverlet

I'm glad I wore my boots. I'm also glad we took the scenic route through the back roads. Come to think of it, that's the only way to get here. The cemetery is actually easy to find during the day, but it would be difficult at night unless you had first located it. Who knows, Ronda might go for a walk during the early evening, but so far, I hadn't seen her.

There appear to be about twenty-five graves, few with inscriptions. Ronda's shouldn't be hard to find. I think we can see it from here—the one above ground. I'm not sure that's hers since the sandstone markers can no longer be read—but it fits the legend's description. Rocks have fallen and broken. Perhaps she doesn't mind or hasn't noticed.

We could speak to her, but she may not answer. "Ronda?" Nothing, just as I suspected. I would think she awakens at night.

So this is her... shall we say *realm*? This is what we came for. I'll take pictures before leaving, just in case her spirit shows on film. Watch your step. You could fall into a larger-than-a-gopher hole.

If Ronda is really a witch, why can't she materialize wildflowers all over this place? Maybe she has. Many of these plants appear to be iris, just not yet blooming at the time of our early spring visit.

"Horse-crippler" cactus, less than eleven inches tall, grows in abundance. In summer this prolific cactus puts forth tight pink blooms, creating a colorful landscape Ronda may have planned. It may stop large animals from encroaching on her domain, but it would not bother Ronda one bit, her being a witch and all.

At the entrance to the cemetery, a tall rusty gate stands, padlocked. It joins a fence with two rows of barbed wire on top. The only car we've seen driving by so far is the sheriff's. Better wave at him.

I've heard *some* spirits actually follow you home. We'd best leave to have you back before dark.

The visit to Ronda Cemetery was worth the three hundred miles, however, I did drop my keys somewhere in the cactus. I was lucky to find them where I attempted to climb over the fence. After scooping them up I turned for a final look at the grave. It was a fine visit, but I probably won't return to the scene of the climb.

Goodnight now, Ronda. Rest well.

A Moss-Covered Grave

Mary Joe Clendenin of Erath County shares this tale from her book *Galloping Ghosts*. The original article, written by her father, Joe Fitzgerald, appeared in the Stephenville paper in 1936.

The events transpired on Halloween, but only because it happened to be on that date. It could have occurred any night, any year. This one took place in the 1870s.

First, let us begin with the setting: A white-steepled church nestled among rolling green hills. The graveyard used by many families for as many years was nearby. A creek spanned by a narrow footbridge separated the church and graveyard. The visual would make a beautiful painting for remembrance.

A small number of people formed the community, and children of different ages attended a one-room schoolhouse. It may or may not have been painted red. Whatever the color, surely a little girl with braids sat in front of a freckled-face boy, who dipped a braid in his inkwell more than once. Maybe a boy even put a frog in the teacher's desk. That is, when the stream was not dry and frogs splashed in the water.

Remember, the time of our story was near Halloween. Some of the "older" young people gathered at one of their homes. They had enjoyed an evening of candy making and began making plans for the Halloween school party.

As the legend goes, they huddled in front of the fireplace, the only heat of the times. Taking turns, they presented ideas for the party's festivities and rejected a repeat of a tacky party from the year before. They looked forward to a longer party this Halloween. "Past midnight," the teacher had said.

The party would be full of activities from a spelling bee and picnic supper to a singing. Singings were important functions, and young people looked forward to participating.

But back to the scary part of the tale. One of the boys in the group of young people suggested they go to the graveyard. Another said that wouldn't be scary because they walked by it all the time.

Again a voice piped up saying they walked past the graveyard during the day, but maybe after dark it would be frightening. They decided to draw numbers to see who would be the "lucky" one to go to the graveyard at midnight.

It happened a girl named Cynthia, who was one of the prettiest ones in the group, could not get past her fear of being the chosen one. A friend offered to take her place, should Cynthia win—or lose—as the case may be. The number selection was drawn out over several days, to build tension. Someone said a corpse rises from the grave on Halloween.

Cynthia became more nervous as each day passed.

Someone else said a ghost lived under the old footbridge. As if that were not enough, one of the boys said, "A bony hand reaches out of the grave and grabs anyone who disturbs it!"

The final day came for the drawing, and Cynthia was frantic for fear the drawn number would be hers. Her fears were founded. She was the one to go!

Some of her friends thought she might never get there at all. She took a fork with her to dig moss from the grave, proving she had actually been to the graveyard. Toward evening's end, Cynthia gathered her courage, knowing if she didn't get started, she might never go at all.

As she hurried across the footbridge, the shadows cast by the trees seemed longer. Of course, Cynthia had never been on such a venture before. The shadows probably were no longer on this night, but they did seem to be dancing across the gravestones, stopping when Cynthia arrived at the chosen site covered with moss.

The strange and eerie noises drifting through the graveyard melded into some sort of strident chords. An owl's screech added an exclamation point. Cynthia scarcely heard, so intent she was on her task. She knelt by the grave and thrust the fork into the moss. The tines could barely penetrate the hard soil. Again, she jabbed at the ground—again and again.

Sobbing, she remembered her friends had told her if she couldn't go through with it, to go on home and they would see her the next morning.

"Go home!" That is what she wanted to do. Just get out of this place that terrorized her so. Trembling, Cynthia got up on one knee but could go no farther. She pulled and pulled, trying to rise, but the bony fingers from the grave held her close.

Cynthia's friends waited hours for her return then decided she had gone home after all. But she never made it home.

Early the next morning, they found her lying dead across the grave. The fork had pierced her clothing, holding her tightly to the moss-covered grave.

All legends are told in several forms and the above is another. They can all have the same general storyline with different embellishments and some are even based on true events. Whatever their origins, these legends have traveled far and wide.

Who knows how many place settings out there are minus a fork?

Up a Tree

Is it on a plane? Is it in a car? What, it's in a tree?

After hearing some stories through the years, we eventually think there might be something to what we have heard. If our thoughts are strong enough, we want to see for ourselves, or at least talk with people who vow they are true.

Bowie, Texas, named after Alamo hero James Bowie has been a thriving town in Montague County since its beginning in 1882. Settlers had scattered in the area for two decades, but after the Fort Worth and Denver Railway came, they moved right to where the action was.

North Texas is loaded with trees—pecan, oak, and mesquite. In the 1800s, oak trees were synonymous with ropes, although a hangin' is not a part of this tale. Somehow, most of the trees lack personality, with one tree the exception. The special tree in this story grows in a small graveyard called Briar Creek.

Driving from north or south on Highway 287 to Bowie, turn west on 59 toward Jacksboro. Drive about four miles to FM 2583 and turn left. Briar Creek Cemetery is less than a mile, just over a slight hill, north of Selma Park.

There is no way of knowing the identity of the ghost-woman who is a victim of insomnia in Briar Creek Cemetery. It is not

Now you see her, now you don't

certain if she had even lived in Bowie. The fact remains—there is an eerie tale here.

Different people have reported seeing the ethereal form of a woman sitting in a tree in this little cemetery.

Occasionally a story turns up that examines our own rationale, even though paranormally speaking, it could be true. The ghost-woman might have been frightened. The question is what would frighten a ghost? Spiders and gophers and snakes? Oh my!

It is said in order to see the ghost in the tree, one must be at Briar Creek at midnight. That appears to be her selected time for ascension. We might wonder what she is doing up there in the first place. If it's December, she could be looking for Christmas wraiths.

Chapter 3

Texas Cemeteries

The most common burial ground in America was the churchyard, at least through the close of the nineteenth century. This followed the early custom of Europe.

In Europe, burial within the church was preferred. Once the church was full, the outside garden took over. Or under. An ancestor of mine is buried beneath the beautiful marble floor of a church in London, but his wife had to accept being interred outside the window. That's less than shouting distance.

In America, after the Civil War, most burials were required to take place outside the town's limits. Remember, no embalming, so apparently six feet below was not enough.

In early Texas, as in other rural areas across the country, most burials took place on a family's farmland, or often where the person fell dead. The shovel had to be sharp and the grave deep, so wild animals wouldn't investigate.

A crude wooden cross might have marked the site where a child died of disease, before the family continued their wagon journey. They would never be back to place flowers on the grave or stand beside it to say another prayer.

For family survivors who belonged to the church, they had only to pay the cost of grave digging. Since this was the sole expense for burial, no additional funds were available for upkeep. If the family eventually moved away, the preacher might try to remove the weeds around gravesites but would soon discontinue. When a small town or community dissolved, no one remained as caretakers. A ghost could resent that.

Cemeteries in America were the final outgrowth of individual burial places near homes of the earliest settlers. In Texas, burial grounds adjacent to a church are not obsolete, but the tradition began to wane when church graveyards grew into disrepair because of the neglect.

Nowhere can a person absorb more history and tradition of his own state than in a small country graveyard.

Various cemeteries are maintained by organizations including Masonic fraternities, historical societies, or groups of concerned citizens. Garden cemeteries are prevalent, frequently owned by the city. Occasionally, a caring property owner might keep up a small family burial spot, never knowing those who once lived on his land.

Save the Cemeteries, Inc., an organization founded in Texas in 1996, has done much to clean up and protect abandoned graveyards in the state. Thanks to this organization and historical societies, as well as caring individuals, this can be accomplished.

Desecration of cemeteries by living "lost souls" is still taking place. One day this sick practice will be a thing of the past. A single word can solve it all: Respect.

Many Texas counties can now boast no neglected cemeteries within their borders. Parker County, for instance, has completed cleanup of its last known "lost" cemetery and hopes to keep them all in good condition.

Still, neglected graveyards are found across the state. They don't have to be old to be haunted, but the years do give more time to accumulate restless spirits.

Many graveyards have disappeared into near-oblivion in the center of a pasture. When driving down the highway, you might see a grove of trees and brush way out in the field, quite possibly hiding an abandoned graveyard.

If the landowner chooses to use the land for farming, he must first move all the graves to another location, identifying each site

An abandoned graveyard

with its original marker. The farmer may as well let the departed rest in peace where they lie.

Would our deceased ancestors experience the same frustration as we do when relocating? The Corps of Engineers have moved gravesites to another location when lakes or railroad tracks are needed. Do they always move them, or does a train with its whistle blowin' in the wind rattle our ancestors' bones every time it rumbles down the track? Good enough reason for a spirit to climb out of its grave. Talk about insomnia!

In one North Texas graveyard, only the stones were removed while a commercial development covered the land and remains of those interred. Workers in another abandoned cemetery moved all the stones alongside a fence so they could mow the weeds. Unfortunately, they made no notation as to which sites the stones belonged.

Mausoleums, on the other hand, always seem to make their whereabouts known. They are more than a tradition in our state. The first Texas mausoleum was built in Sherman at a cost of $100,000 in 1921 and is located in West Hill Cemetery. Marcia K. Rolbiecki of the Red River Historical Museum shared information concerning the mausoleum's Tiffany stained-glass triptych window. The glorious central panel is titled "The Angel of Truth," an angel in a flowing white robe. Were it to be replaced, the window is valued at half the original cost of the building.

The Angel of Truth
Courtesy of the Red River Historical Museum

Why do people visit cemeteries? The first answer might be to pay respects to a loved one. Second is for genealogical research to check birth and death dates or to accomplish a little stone rubbing. Before the turn of the nineteenth century, markers were referred to as gravestones.

Other reasons exist for visiting cemeteries: photographing, recording clever epitaph inscriptions, bringing flowers on special occasions, or simply to enjoy the quiet. I won't leave out ghost hunting. Above all, respect is due the dead.

My great-grandmother Permelia Hawkins, who lived in Somervell County, saved over two hundred letters in the late 1800s. She wrote of her son's death from tuberculosis in 1889: "Our dear Willie was laid to rest beneath a branching tree. It is a peaceful place where sometimes birds sing and flowers grow all over."

If Willie's spirit ever took ghostly form, he would probably see wildflowers in full bloom.

Lost graveyards, before being refound, might be in full bloom, too. They can be so overgrown a person could scarcely find a way inside. One rainy day I ventured into a cemetery that had its last interment in the late 1880s. Nothing ventured, no adventure.

Although it was early afternoon, the thick brush kept out the light. Smaller broken limbs clutched at my clothes. And don't forget the spider webs joining one branch to the next. This was a true experience, not just webbing for a ghost story. As long as I didn't get caught in ectoplasm, I felt safe.

It rained hard that afternoon, but the only drops falling through the trees' thick branches were occasional drippings off climbing poison oak. I took camera shots of overgrowth and fallen headstones, wondering if straightening the latter would be appreciated. And if so, by whom.

Incidentally, don't remove a glove to wipe leaves off a stone. I would not admit I didn't want to get my glove dirty, and that I wiped off poison oak with my bare hand.

If you know of an apparent abandoned graveyard, you might bring it to the attention of your area's historical society. You could also notify Save the Texas Cemeteries, Inc. on the Internet. They would like to know about it.

Chapter 4

Central Texas

Even the Walls Have Spheres

It is said an iron fence keeps evil spirits out of a cemetery. That's what they say. It may be difficult to believe, considering the subject of this story.

For 150 years, the foreboding red brick prison in downtown Huntsville has been open to, then closed after, those who have been sentenced to serve time.

The Walls Unit of Huntsville houses 1,600 inmates. The colorful history of Huntsville prisons has proved an important basis for the modern Texas Department of Criminal Justice. Unfortunately, not all inmates face eventual freedom in the outside world as we know it—but perhaps to an outside world known only to vaporous beings. Should prisoners reach their demise while serving a sentence, and no one claims them, their remains are interred within an iron-fenced prison cemetery.

According to a 1999 *Dallas Morning News* article, the Huntsville cemetery named after Captain Joe Byrd, has served as inmates' resting place for many years; however, there are those who say not all inmates are resting.

Over the years shadowy black hearses have pulled up to the Joe Byrd Cemetery, carrying a plywood box containing the remains of the recently deceased prisoner. One member of the burial detail comments, "Dust to dust, just as the good Lord says."

The chaplain believes many people could find no better place to be buried. The nineteen acres have a "lush carpet of grass, blooming red roses and soaring pines."

Inmates give perpetual care to the pristine cemetery. It has been reserved for prisoners since the 1800s and contains as many as 1,700 graves. There may be more, except aged markers have disappeared.

According to legend, in this garden of stone, discontented ghostly apparitions wander through the nineteen acres, as well as in the building itself. About fifty years ago, the practice of placing names on the markers had been abolished, with only prisoners' numbers on the handcrafted crosses. It seemed a good idea when the warden recently decided to reinstate placing names on the markers—The spheres might forget their addresses.

The chaplain states, "We don't have to fear death. We don't have to be afraid to pass from this life into the next." However, in the paranormal world, this is not always true of those who questioned their behavior on earth.

There is not a steady stream of daily visitors to the cemetery. That might be a different story if you were to venture too close at night.

If you think about it, cemetery ghosts don't have to be confined behind bars. Bars do not a prison make.

Mike Ward, staff-writer for the *American-Statesman*, interviewed a prison worker who never believed the tales he had heard about prison ghosts. We'll call him Luke, to protect his privacy.

Luke hadn't known whether to believe a story his father, also a former corrections officer, had told him about a harrowing experience. One night while at his desk, Luke became aware of a movement from the corner of his eye. Looking up, he viewed a dark figure, not clearly outlined, walking down the hallway. It occurred to him the form came from the wall, not the hallway itself.

No convict was supposed to be in the hall at that time, so he got up from his paperwork and followed the figure. It walked right through a cell door. According to the lone inmate in the cell, the "thing" came through the bars and out the back wall.

Luke became a believer.

Seguin's Ghost

S eguin in the springtime is one of the most beautiful areas in the state. Wildflowers drape the countryside, and after an April rain, the landscape looks silvery-white.

If you are wandering through the old Seguin Cemetery, the silvery-white you catch a glimpse of may not be a product of the rain. It is said—and people have seen it—a headless ghost walks nearby.

Seguin is the county seat of Guadalupe County, thirty-five miles northeast of San Antonio. The history is vast, rich in soil and minerals. It has been an archaeological dream, with the discovery of remains of mammoths and Indian villages. After the early 1700s, Spanish, Mexican, and Angelo settlements were founded.

Seguin became a town in the 1840s and kept right on growing. By the Civil War, its citizens raised cattle and hogs. They prospered, growing peanuts, cotton, and corn. When the war ended, Union soldiers occupied the town.

The Seguin Cemetery is only three blocks from downtown and is situated on sloping ground with a few trees offering shades minimal shade. The graveyard is not especially picturesque, as you might imagine it would be. It is old. And reportedly haunted.

If you visit what people would like to call hallowed ground, pay particular attention to where you have just been and use your peripheral vision wisely. Granted, you are not out in the country. You are in town, close to other humans—and some perhaps not so human.

According to John Troesser, editor of *Texas Escapes*, the story was related to him by author Charles Eckhardt. A headless ghost has been seen walking down Milam Street, away from the cemetery.

Milam Street curves, but the ghost does not follow the curve. He has a path all his own, continuing toward the railroad tracks. The headless creature walks along the tracks then disappears.

Local legend tells us he was a Confederate soldier, decapitated in a sword or bayonet altercation, and is searching for his head. Of course he would.

However, the fact the ghost progresses toward the railroad tracks gives credence to another theory that he worked for the railroad and lost his head when run over by a train.

When the ghost eventually disappeared by the tracks, it seemed to dissolve into that silvery mist people reported seeing and apparently returned to its place in the graveyard. None of the witnesses said they observed the ghost's return, just that the ghost always left his grave.

It has long been believed that dogs and horses can sense the presence of ghosts. In this story, dogs have been known to bark incessantly when the apparition passed by. If their masters tried to quiet the animals, they would cower as the apparition continued down his path.

The story relates the headless ghost was known to detour, appearing in someone's home, merely passing through. Nothing was taken or touched, nor was anyone spoken to. The residents may have frozen in their tracks for an instant, but no permanent harm was done.

If Union soldiers ever occupied the area, and our soldier-ghost was Confederate, he may have been trying all these years to catch the next train out of town. He didn't wish to remain with the boys in blue.

On August 18, 1988, Seguin celebrated its sesquicentennial year, but the headless ghost paid no attention to such celebrations. He had more important things to worry about, such as finding his head.

Footprints in the Sand

The small community of Bald Prairie is two miles east of Twin Oak Reservoir in the northeast corner of Robertson County. It got its name from the open prairie, thought by the settlers to be undesirable for farming. They decided they could grow crops along banks of creeks and streams, which they did. But in time they wanted to try higher ground. Surprisingly, the upper land proved to be favorable for cotton and corn, and livestock didn't seem to mind either.

Not much is left of Bald Prairie. The railroad was mostly to blame for the area's decline since the tracks bypassed the community. Records of 1990 indicate a few scattered houses remained, along with a couple churches and a cemetery.

The writing was in the sand about 1890 when Emily, a friend of my great-grandmother Permelia Hawkins, wrote her a letter concerning the slowing economy of the little town. In the letter, she tells of a tragedy that forms a fitting tale for this book.

> Bald Prairie
> Robertson Co. Texas
> February 5, 1890

Dear Sister Hawkins and family,

After long delay I seat myself to answer your letter which was most kind and welcome. I hope you will not be angry with me for not writing before now. I was waiting for my daughters Lou and Annie to get their pictures taken to send to your girls.... Thank you so much for inviting me down to see you before we go to New Mexico. I hate to leave, but things are not so good here any longer....

....We had a tragic thing happen just recently. There was a woman killed by a man only five miles from here. This man went to their house and saw no one at home except the woman. Her husband was working in a field a mile away.

After the man killed her, he took all the clothing he could find, piled it on top of her, and poured coal oil all over it. He then set it on fire, thinking it would burn the house. It burned her clothes off and burned one or two holes in the floor and then went out.

Her husband smelled the smoke and went rushing back to the house. He got some men together who were working in the field and they tracked the man down. They caught him and brought him back to measure his tracks in the sandy dirt with his shoes, and they were the same size. He finally acknowledged that he was the one that killed her.

They got him to the law and started to Franklin with him in a hack. There was about a hundred men who surrounded the hack and wouldn't let it go on. They took the man out and hung him, and shot him full of holes and left him hanging there on the tree. Next day, some folks got to thinking and went out and buried him right there. Tell me what your thoughts are....

Emily

Apparently my great-grandmother answered her friend because the following are quotes from Emily's next letter which she wrote less than ten days later.

Dear Sister Hawkins,

....About the man who got hung. I can't tell you how some people have reacted to such a thing. But after maybe a week passed, a man who was one of them that hung him declared he saw this man up and walking around that tree one night. He had one shoe on and was carrying the other one. Then someone else that wasn't even there for the hanging, vowed he saw him still swinging from the tree. And he is no drinker either.

The girls are right scared. Some think it might be a ghost... I tell you, I don't know what to think....

There are cemeteries in Robertson County, but according to Emily, this "cemetery for one" was five miles from Bald Prairie. That isn't much to go on—finding a grave and a tree used for a hanging more than a century ago. Adding five miles to a circle around what used to be Bald Prairie in 1890 might lead us to the barefooted ghost of the killer. How patient can you be?

Analyzing it, the ghost may have been taking off his shoes so his tracks could not be compared to those left at the burned house. He didn't think about his bare feet leaving prints, but by that time he was probably a little out of it.

As for the other man's story about seeing him swinging from the tree? Maybe the woman's killer just likes to...hang out.

Seven Vandals

Schulenburg, Texas, has a rich musical heritage. In the past it has boasted several orchestras as well as the "Gold Chain Bohemian Band." Austrians, Czechs, and Germans settled the area in the 1850s, bringing with them their own artistic musical talent. Music did not cause the prosperity, however. Perseverance and hard work did, along with many early commercial businesses.

Once again, it can be said a railroad helped create a town. Schulenburg was founded in 1873 after the railroad came through. Louis Schulenburg donated land for the railroad, so the respectful thing to do was name the town after him.

The community boasted four newspapers around the turn of the twentieth century. Think of the columnists who could have written tales of haunted graveyards!

One of the oldest graveyards in town is referred to as Lyons Cemetery, named after Warren Lyons, who was reported killed by Indians. At least that's what the stonecutter chiseled on Warren's marker.

Oops, so what can you do when it's "carved in stone?" Warren Lyons was not killed after all! The Indians had killed his father instead. The truth is, the younger Lyons was captured and raised by the Comanches. There is now a state marker with the correction for all to see.

Since Warren's original gravesite still occupies a plot in the cemetery, it seems reasonable his ghost might occasionally appear at the empty grave. So far, no one has reported seeing Warren Lyons, and this story is not about his ghost.

This strange tale concerns seven young vandals who had nothing better to do than damage the graveyard.

The legend says the boys were later found hanging from the rafters of a barn close to the cemetery. This was a long time ago, mind you, when hangings occurred almost as the norm. It would have taken more than one person to accomplish that deed, and so far, no one has discovered who carried out the boys' punishment.

If you want to venture into Lyons Cemetery, Schulenburg is eighteen miles south of La Grange in southern Fayette County. It is at the intersection of Interstate 10, Highway 77, and Farm Road 1579.

Remember if you go at night, which is the choice time for seeing ghostly activity, you might catch a glimpse of seven apparitions. Perhaps they would be straightening gravestones and neatening the place. Surely they have not been hanging around all these years, having learned nothing.

Some residents of Schulenburg know the tale of the seven vandals. No doubt about it, there is something shady going on around there.

Out for a Swim

Kelly Ehlinger tells of an experience both intriguing and harrowing. This occurrence took place near the restful town of Wimberley.

Many vacation spots dot the Texas Hill Country where bald cypress and pecan trees line the riverbanks. Summer activities pick up with tourists flocking to its July rodeo and weekly flea markets. Delicate maidenhair ferns grow in the limestone banks of flowing creeks over which oak trees tower.

The clear Cypress Creek is a popular place for swimming and perfect for a family respite. Vacationers stop for a happy weekend or longer at the campground bound on one side by an aged rock wall. A narrow dirt road is on the other side, opposite an old cemetery with gravestones dating from over a century ago.

Kelly and her family have often strolled through the cemetery in the evening, envisioning the lives of the dead who may have once walked where they now did. She wondered if those people ever really swam in Cypress Creek or jumped from the banks into the clean cool water. One evening after Kelly, her husband, and two other couples had enjoyed a long day of swimming and picnicking, the three women decided to have a moonlight swim in a spot they had heard about. A tributary from the stream angled off into an enticing pool of crystalline water. They climbed over the stone wall and began walking the short distance to the pool, almost pretending they were kids again, rushing off to the ol' swimming hole.

The night didn't turn out to be as moonlit as they had expected. Only the stars broke through, leaving the moon somewhere behind a cloud. Nevertheless, they looked forward to their private outing without having to watch the children for a little while.

The women enjoyed splashing in their private pool when suddenly they stopped, feeling something unnatural. The air seemed to tighten about them, like it does on a very hot day—almost holding them in one spot. Silence prevailed. Even the crickets must have gone to sleep for the night. Of course not, crickets don't sleep at night. They must have quieted, sensing something sinister.

Kelly and her companions felt the same presence. They didn't speak. Maybe a stranger peered at them through the trees. That had to be it. Kelly's first impulse was to run, or at least call for help from their husbands. But the last thing any one of them could do was scream. The water became frigid.

At that instant, three golden spheres rushed down the path from the cemetery like a phantasmagoria of light. The spheres darted toward the women, then swerved, ignoring them while at the same time appearing to want their reaction. The movement of the glowing balls was precise, each identical to the other. They moved so fast, surely they would have made a sound, but no— nothing.

They were not in the water, but skimming above it. As soon as they passed, vanishing, the women stared at each other in silence, each thinking: "How fast can we get out of here?"

They scrambled up the banks, alert enough to grab their clothes, and ran all the way to the stone wall, scraping a shin or two in their hurry to climb over it.

They didn't speak of the experience right away for fear of frightening the children, but they could scarcely wait to tell their husbands.

If you desire to chance a visit to the depths of the crystalline pool, the little resort town of Wimberley is on Farm Road 12, four- teen miles northwest of San Marcos and forty miles southwest of Austin, in western Hays County.

Could the three glowing spheres have been ghosts from the old cemetery, merely playing hide-and-seek among the cypress and oak trees? Or perhaps they were trying to tell their visitors something.

After the founding of Wimberley over a hundred and twenty- five years ago, how many times have the ghosts ventured from their resting place?

What else would silence a cricket?

Who's in the Basement?

If no one is there to hear, is there still a sound?
In my North Texas hometown, only a few houses had basements, and then only if the builder knew his business—something to do with the soil. My parents used theirs for storage. It also contained the water heater and a large furnace.

I digress. This is a story of a different basement. As the dictionary states, a "legend" is a popular story handed down from earlier times. Otherwise, everyone might take the "Legend of Sleepy Hollow" for nothing but the truth.

Near the Salado Creek and Austin Highway on the Old Camino Real is the location of this particular basement and this particular legend. When people passed by the long-abandoned house, they reported hearing sounds of a woman weeping. Some might have said the wind breathing through broken windows caused the cries, but apparently the sobs sounded too real.

It seemed the husband and wife frequently quarreled. Then on one occasion their arguing turned into violent rage, culminating in the man killing his wife.

It seems obvious he didn't know the "rule of thumb." An old English law states a man could not beat his wife with anything wider than his thumb.

Being an individual of intelligence, his first thought was to get rid of the body. Naturally, the basement presented the obvious burial site. Again, being clever, he chose not to hurt his back by carrying his wife. He simply took hold of her feet and pulled her limp form down the flight of stairs, one rung at a time. Her head surely banged against each hard step as she drew nearer the basement.

He dug the grave in the dirt floor and shoved her in; later he covered the floor with quicklime to hide any evidence. If you were ever to pass by this house, providing it still stands; you might hear the woman's cries. Listen for the thump, thump of her head against the steps.

Fanthorp Inn

The grief-stricken woman wandered across the moors. Wait, Texas doesn't have moors! At least not the kind in Bronte's *Wuthering Heights*. Let's start at the beginning and get our apparitions in focus.

In the heart of Grimes County, Fanthorp Inn stands out in history as a hostelry like you might find in Malpas, England, in the seventeenth century. Not in looks perhaps, but in sheer mystique.

Henry Fanthorp built the inn on land he purchased for twenty-five cents an acre. Famous dignitaries like Robert E. Lee and Jefferson Davis stayed there during the 1850s. Fanthorp died in 1867 and the place soon closed, remaining vacant for many years. The amazing fact is most of the original windows are still intact.

The actual location is Anderson, which is on State Highway 90 and Farm Roads 1774 and 149, ten miles northeast of Navasota. The inn became the first post office.

This area was rich with good crops and soil. Stagecoaches rambled across Grimes County, allowing Anderson to become a drawing card for professional men and political leaders. At one time it was the fourth largest town in Texas, even establishing a pistol factory that provided handguns for the Confederacy. The town fairly boomed.

With all Anderson's history, many of its citizens could be responsible for returning as ghosts, but we may never know who or why.

Hunters often roved the grassy bottomlands near Fanthorp Inn. Their hunting took place during the 1930s when it stood vacant. And of course, barking dogs, ready for prey, traveled with them. Strong brave dogs they were, until they suddenly stopped in their tracks and changed their barking to whimpers.

The hunters proceeded through weeds and brush to determine what frightened their animals. The inn's lawn sloped down the hillside where fog engulfed the riders. As they came to an open space, the fog dissipated, allowing them to see the apparition of a woman clad in white, slowly moving across the lawn.

Having no concern for tangled brush, the woman appeared to glide. It seemed to the men she was deeply mournful. However, she mystified them by disappearing, leaving them no chance to investigate further.

Much to the apparent relief of the dogs, the men closed out their hunting trip. Although the hunters had never heard about it at that time, others had reported seeing the crying apparition, most often during bright moonlit nights. The figure moved over the lawn and crossed the road to the family cemetery. She wandered amongst the headstones and finding a specific one, fell to the ground, weeping.

It is said the family who later moved into the inn was aware of unusual noises. If they heard furniture being rearranged or dishes moved from cabinets during the night, no sign of disturbance remained by morning.

The Fanthorp family cemetery and inn have been restored. The inn and some of the downtown area became part of its historic district.

Even if Anderson *did* have English moors, the hunters' hounds probably never heard of the Baskervilles.

Moon Music

A lonely trumpeter plays his cherished instrument, letting his fellow soldiers in the cemetery know he is with them.

Brackettville is a historical spot in our state, besides being the location for a John Wayne movie. And perhaps that in itself is historical.

The community with a population around 2,000 has something other towns of its size do not have: four Congressional Medal of Honor winners. These courageous black men were buried next to each other in Brackettville's Seminole Cemetery. Surrounded by a metal fence, they rest just as they had served—side by side—as "Seminole Negro Indian Scouts" during the Indian Wars of the late 1800s.

Many Black Seminoles were removed to Indian Territory, which in 1907 became the state of Oklahoma. According to William Gwaltney, former park ranger assigned to the Fort Davis National Historic Site in Fort Davis, the group of experienced frontier guerilla fighters was recruited from Mexico in 1870.

The scouts were known as "Mascogos," descendants of runaway slaves and free Africans who joined the Seminole Indians in Florida prior to the Civil War. Some scouts married into Indian tribes. In most of the intermarriages, the non-Indians were required to go through various verbal tests of loyalty, thus becoming Indian by marriage.

The government removed them to Indian Territory, but the Bureau of Indian Affairs did not keep their promises of food and land in Oklahoma. They kept their promises no better than they did to the Arizona Apaches in the late 1800s. Because of poor treatment, they migrated to Mexico. However, the U.S. Military sent General Zenas Bliss across the border to bring back Indian scouts. In effect, "promise them anything."

The eldest member of the above four medal winners was Adam Paine. He was born in 1854 and enlisted at age twenty-eight. John Ward joined at about twenty-three years of age, and the youngest of the group—Pompey Factor and Isaac Payne— joined at seventeen and sixteen.

Again, promises were broken. Yet, almost every superior officer these four men served under marveled at their courage and battle skills.

According to records, they served under Lieutenant John Bullis, a white man who respected their superb tracking ability and loyalty—and well he should. This was reinforced by the actions of Factor, Payne, and Sergeant Ward during an April day in 1875. They were tracking a group of Indians who had stolen seventy-five horses.

The lieutenant and the three scouts, on foot, were outflanked by the Indians, and they made a dash for their horses. Bullis had ridden a just-broken wild horse that had apparently been spooked. It bolted, leaving the lieutenant stranded.

When the scouts realized the horse had disappeared, they rode back through gunfire to rescue their lieutenant. The foursome lucked out, escaping with their lives. The three scouts later received the Medal of Honor for this bravery in the line of fire.

Private Paine received his Medal of Honor for gallantry in action for service to Colonel R.S. Mackenzie, at Staked Plains in 1874. Adam Paine could have been called eccentric inasmuch as he occasionally wore a Comanche buffalo helmet. Seeing him in somewhat of a Walkire attire could be frightening.

The Seminole-Indian Scouts maintained pride in themselves as well as loyalty to the Army. Lieutenant Bullis stayed in command of the scouts until 1881, although the scouts organization continued until the early twentieth century.

Adam Paine was killed by a shotgun blast in his back by a Texas sheriff. The sheriff was later acquitted of the so-called accident, causing Pompey Factor and other scouts to return, disillusioned, to Mexico.

The scouts served at Fort Clark until 1914. An interesting item is that no scout was ever killed or injured in battle. Fort Clark and Brackettville are 120 miles west of San Antonio on U.S. 90 in Kinney County. The Seminole Indian Cemetery is 3.1 miles south of Brackettville on FM Road 3348.

Inscribed on the cemetery's Historical Marker of the State of Texas: "Burial site of heroic U.S. Army men, families, and heirs, these Seminoles came mainly from Florida about 1850; lived in Northern Mexico or Texas; Joined Lieutenant (later a general) John L. Bullis and Colonel Ranald S. Mackenzie in ridding Texas of hostile Indians, 1870s."

Trumpeter Isaac Payne, Adam Paine, Pompey Factor, and John Ward are interred in graves surrounded by a white metal fence.

Isaac was born in Mexico. Legend indicates he was captured as a boy and raised by Comanches. The soldiers captured the Comanches, thereby freeing Isaac. Soon after, he enlisted. Being musically inclined, Isaac became trumpeter for his unit.

The Seminole Cemetery has an air of peace about it. Deserved peace came long after bias and racial prejudices had been cast upon the Seminole Scouts. It's a grand old cemetery, and the gravestone inscriptions are poignant.

If you visit the cemetery as many tourists do, wait until late evening when the moon is up. You may hear the young private, Isaac Payne, playing his trumpet, reminding you that he and the other one hundred scouts are at peace.

The Other Half

The Giddings City Cemetery is just west of town on Highway 290. It has two unpaved entrances, and if you choose to visit, it is safer to enter from the street bordering the cemetery on the east. Safe from what? I forgot to ask.

Nothing dangerous has occurred in this large cemetery. Well, that isn't altogether true. Gunslinger Bill Longley found his final resting place on this earth in Giddings.

One death sentence by hanging was brought about through guilt by association, similar to Jake in McMurtry's *Lonesome Dove*. Longley escaped the rope another time by a stroke of fate, or stroke of gunfire, when the rope was severed in the nick of time. As yet, no one has reported seeing his ghost swing from a noose.

Robert L. Ripley reported that Longley had three rope escapes. Believe it or not because Longley actually made it the third try to the gallows. To and fro, as in swinging. He and John Wesley Hardin may be reminiscing right now about their wayward ways.

Enough about Bill Longley. It's easy to get sidetracked, but you never know when you'll dig up a ghost.

Giddings Cemetery still holds a puzzling enigma that may or may not have an answer.

John Troesser has a historical interest in old graveyards. He chose a cold day to take some shots of interesting headstones, but for the sake of this tale, he regretted it wasn't a dark and stormy night. Personally, I think he was overjoyed that he had only the cold to deal with. He may have been dealing with something other than the weather and just didn't know it.

This is a cemetery which has several graves with porcelain photos mounted in the headstone. You don't see many of these any more, depending on the tradition of the area. John noticed one such photo of a rather stern-looking young man. After clicking the shutter, he noticed another interesting one. He shot with his close-up lens, about sixteen inches away from the stone, expecting great results.

John took his twenty-four-exposure roll of film and after developing it, found all but two prints to be well centered and clear. The remaining two? Both were the men's photos. Although he knew he had centered them equally well, only three-quarters of their images, cut vertically, showed up in the final photograph. To have two separate prints with the same problem seemed an unlikely coincidence.

No problem, he would stop by Giddings another day, preferably a sunny afternoon. John took twenty-four more shots of other headstones, including the two that did not turn out the first time.

He is no amateur; he's been into photography several years. John took special care in focusing so the faces would be *dead* center.

When John shuffled through the finished prints, he stopped at the two photographs. A chill shot through him as he glanced at the first, then the second. Both were only half-faces, but this time, cut horizontally.

Mrs. Troesser suggested her husband not try a third time. He tended to agree that the two subjects did not want their images removed from the gravestones. Every time he looked at the prints, he shivered.

Perhaps a third try would bring no picture at all.

Chapter 5

East Texas

Athens' Catacombs

Some cemeteries are buried. In the movie version of Daphne du Maurier's *Don't Look Now*, a tiny character dressed in a red-hooded cape and carrying a dagger ran through an underpass next to the canals of Venice. Actor Donald Sutherland chased the form, thinking it was his deceased daughter. He was dead wrong. Mr. Sutherland should have stayed topside.

Athens, Texas, the "Black-eyed Pea Capital of the World," is a long way from the canals of Italy. The town got its start in 1850. A cotton gin, brick plant, hotel, newspaper, and bank came into being during the last half of the nineteenth century. Today it is a proud city with Trinity Valley Community College, manufacturing companies, and friendly people.

Many residents believe the story of Athens' underground catacombs was manufactured by an imaginative legend-maker. Hence, this tale brings us to the town's Fuller Park, named after the Rev. Melton Lee Fuller, a beloved Baptist preacher who died in 1944.

Brian Spurling of Athens wrote a 1989 article for the *Athens Review*, in which he describes the park and its lore. A network of tunnels is believed by some to run beneath portions of the city.

The talk of such tunnels gains importance during Halloween. Ancestors of current residents have passed down their versions of the mysterious Fuller Park. One resident advised the *Athens Review* that her aunt said tunnels similar to those in coal mines were used in the 1800s by slaves who fled the South.

The same person said her aunt accompanied friends many years past to the site where one portion of a tunnel was reported. They finally found the entry door, flat on the ground and covered with leaves. Since the young woman was afraid, she waited outside while the others lifted the door and cautiously entered.

Her companions returned, free at least for the time being of a reported curse akin to that of entering a pharaoh's tomb. They delivered the ghostly news of having discovered strange markings and pentagrams painted on the walls, as well as scattered bones in the underground tunnel area.

It is said the entrance and one exit are now filled and boarded closed. Since the openings were parallel to the ground, it would be next to impossible to locate them.

Have I mentioned the Fuller Park Cemetery yet? No? Mr. and Mrs. Fuller were buried in one area designated for a family cemetery. They had no children, and Mr. Fuller's will was assumed to have been burned in a fire near the time of his death. That in itself seemed mysterious.

A 1987 park survey indicated the possibility of more graves than had previously been noted. Several depressions in the soil appeared near the sites of the Rev. Fuller and his wife, Virginia.

Historians find the tunnel theory less than plausible. Tunneling would have to be through sand, particularly since the water table is so high.

Late-night workers in the area have told of strange sounds emitting from the cemetery at odd hours.

And what about that curious roofed arbor, known as the "monkey cages"? Again, versions and rumors surrounding the cages prevailed. Many years ago, were monkeys or wild beasties of another sort contained therein? Could noises the night workers heard have been the howl of a ghostly...I guess not.

Van Buren District Library - Covert Branch
33680 M-140 Hwy
Covert MI 49043
269-764-1298   VBDL org

Receipt - 1/26/2018

Van Buren District Library

Items Checked Out Today:
Ghosts in the graveyard : Texas cemetery tales
35101511351368   Due: 2/16/2018

The world's creepiest places
35101512994406   Due: 2/16/2018

New GED : strategies, practice & review
35101513244223   Due: 2/16/2018

Download from the Library! Check your device"s App Store
for Overdrive, Hoopla, and Freegal or visit VBDL.org and
click the eLibrary dropdown menu.

No matter how many tales one hears about Fuller Park, at least a short tunnel apparently ran underground in the last century—perhaps not the labyrinth that has been talked about for so many decades; however, strange sightings have been reported.

Should you decide one night to visit the large dark area of Fuller Park, don't go alone. I'm not saying there is one, but stay clear of a tiny maniacal figure in a red cape, rushing through the wooded area.

Barrett's Blue Light

In 1890 the merchants of Gray Rock in western Titus County refused to donate money and land so the railroad could be routed through their community.

W.C. Barrett came to the rescue, deeding some of his land a mile northeast of Gray Rock, for the railroad. The new town was formed, first named after Mr. Barrett then eventually, Winfield. Once the railroad came, all those merchants who earlier refused to cooperate began moving their businesses to Winfield.

According to a May 1998 article in the *East Texas Journal*, the town's graveyard was known as Barrett Cemetery. It developed a reputation as a spooky place for boys to take their dates.

In the article, a young woman tells of her experience with her date and a group of friends. They were not apt to forget the fright of a warm summer evening. Glenda said one of the boys was the "nervous" type, so the other boys decided to take him to the graveyard for a good scare.

One boy would dress up like a werewolf and hide behind the headstones. The others would go back for scaredy-cat Bob (fictitious), and when the werewolf appeared, they would all have great fun at Bob's expense.

The plan was in order. They arrived at their destination just after dark. The moon, trying to be full, edged from behind a cloud. A werewolf *needed* a full moon.

Out of the cheerless depths of the old graveyard, a blue light appeared, small at first, then increasing in size. It is understandable how the boys might have been petrified. Instead, without being asked, their legs transported them to the car in what would be considered the nick of time.

After they returned to town and settled down, they found clubs for weapons—maybe a baseball bat or two—and planned a return trip. Their skeptical dates were anxious to go along this time to see for themselves.

In the road by the graveyard, the girls peered from the car windows but saw nothing unusual. A couple of the boys, weapons in hand, mustered courage to exit the vehicle and cross the road to the graveyard. It was apparently easier to muster courage than to put it to use.

No sooner had they entered the grounds, than the blue light again appeared. The girls screamed and the boys dashed to the car, the mysterious blue light erupting in swift pursuit. Fortunately the car started at the first turn of the key.

A story of the strange phenomenon circulated through the small town of Winfield like a country party line.

The couples in this tale were not the only ones frightened by the blue light of Barrett Cemetery. Others also reported similar experiences.

No one seemed to have an explanation for the light. Could it be the guilty spirit of someone who did not contribute for the railroad? Or perhaps it's the generous Mr. Barrett hanging around, keeping watch after the graveyard bearing his name.

After Dark

Mothers will do anything to make their children more comfortable—even in death. This loving mother is said to have lived in Kilgore in the days of lanterns.

Kilgore, in Gregg County, was founded in 1872 after the railroad bypassed New Danville. Constantine Buckly Kilgore sold the townsite to the railroad, thus creating the town. Citizens of New Danville could not resist the prospect of a new and thriving community. They moved their businesses, lock, stock, and future ghost to Kilgore.

The town continued to grow until the Great Depression took its toll, forcing businesses to close. That little ol' pest the boll weevil had found its way from the South to northeast Texas, making a meal of the unsuspecting cotton plants. Kilgore had largely depended on the crop for its economy.

As soon as the decline arrived, East Texas discovered oil, transforming Kilgore to a boomtown. The incoming humanity resembled the California Gold Rush. In the early 1930s one downtown block boasted the largest number of oil derricks in the world, labeling the area the "World's Richest Acre."

Pirtle Cemetery lies on another acre in Kilgore—no oil derricks but a large number of gravestones.

This cemetery is the resting place for a young boy. According to legend, he was afraid of the dark. Many children were, but this child was excessively frightened. It is said that his mother left the lamplight on until he fell asleep. If he awakened during the night, he called for his mother. She came to comfort him and relit the lamp.

Sadly, the child became ill, growing weaker by the day. The doctor could do nothing, and the boy did not recover.

During the burial service, his mother thought of his fear of the dark and how he wanted the lamp left on. She had only one thought in her mind—she would carry a lantern to her son's grave at night. He would not be afraid then.

Leave the lamplight burning

In time the mother died. Without her there was no one to keep the lamp on for the little boy. But the light *is* still on.

It is said a flickering flame can be seen in the graveyard at certain times after dark. Perhaps the mother's spirit is making her child comfortable—even in death.

Chicken Wing and the Headless Ghost

"**C**hicken Wing" was a nickname of course, and I don't know how the young man became labeled with it. Even after this story has unfolded, I'm not at all sure he could be called "chicken." Anyone else would probably have reacted the same.

A number of years ago, Chicken Wing was riding his gray horse, Sparky, down a lane off a farm to market road just out of

Tyler. People called it Smith Lane because Smith family members lived in their respective houses on this road, and everybody in the area knew them.

As Sparky loped alongside an old cemetery, he suddenly slowed. Snuffling, he turned his head to the right then left, making it known he didn't want to continue. That horse just applied the brakes and halted. Chicken Wing urged him onward, but the animal neighed and refused.

Sparky rarely needed kicking since he always seemed to know what his master wanted and complied. But on this occasion Chicken put his heel into the horse's side and yelled, "Sparky! C'mon, boy!"

No matter how hard he tried to get him to move, Sparky reared back and pawed the air, like in old cowboy movies. The night stilled and Chicken Wing heard faint sounds in the gravel lane. He turned around and spied a dark form coming out of the cemetery. It said nothing, but a peculiar feeling draped over the young man.

The moon slipped from behind a cloud and Chicken got a good look. He couldn't believe what he saw. He felt transported to Sleepy Hollow, as if he were reading the legend back in grade school. A headless form began running toward them.

Sparky whinnied, flinching when his master jabbed him once more in the side. He took off this time and would have run straight into the barbed wire fence if Chicken hadn't reined him away from it. Even so, he galloped like lightning down the fence line, away from the apparition.

Chicken Wing was as nervous as his horse. He kept looking back, seeing the unbelievable form chasing them. When he glanced the last time, it had disappeared. At least it had disappeared from view.

The terrified horse finally made it to flat land at the bottom of the hill. Sparky didn't slow again until they reached the house. He had worked up a lather and had a walleyed look.

Chicken Wing was out of breath himself, as if he had done the running. He reined his horse and dashed inside. After collecting himself, he returned with caution to the front porch and to Sparky.

He looked around and could see no sign of the specter having followed them.

The horse remained tense, but Chicken Wing walked him to the barn, rubbed him down, and stayed there until he calmed.

Later the young man got up nerve to talk to his family about his experience with the headless ghost. He was surprised to learn he was not the first to have met up with the apparition.

His cousin had the same encounter a few years earlier. He had been walking down the lane past the cemetery toward home when he became aware of someone in back of him. The night was dark and he couldn't see well.

He spoke to whoever approached from behind but got no answer. This irritated him a bit because he thought it was probably one of his cousins.

"Hey, I said it's a nice night, isn't it?" he said. Again, he received no answer. When he looked over his shoulder, he came close to expiring on the spot. The form had no head. He gave up thinking someone was playing a trick on him. Running for his life was the only thought in his mind.

The headless figure chased him as it later chased Chicken Wing.

By the time the teenager rushed through the front door to his home, his hysteria had turned into hyperventilation, concerning his mother enough that she drove him to the hospital. It was only later he told her what happened. He didn't want to talk about it for fear of being ridiculed.

These stories came to me from reliable sources, the first from a man who at one time lived on Smith Lane, and from his cousin who told the second tale. The latter's mother verified the episode. The stories haven't been related so much that they lost much in the original telling.

But one thing I know. It isn't wise to pass too close to the old cemetery when the moon is barely visible.

Keep your wits about you. Don't lose your head.

Diamonds Are Not Forever

The 1840s founders of Jefferson, Texas, might be astounded to learn that *their* town now has the distinct reputation of being the most haunted town in the state. Nestled by Big Cypress Creek and Caddo Lake, with Spanish moss swaying from cypress trees, Jefferson has its own built-in haunted setting. So far no one has reported a creature from the dank waters.

Our special cemetery ghost of this legend is reported to frequent the Excelsior House, the second-oldest house in Jefferson. The Jessie Allen Wise Garden Club restored it in 1961.

The many ghosts wandering through its halls and rooms probably appreciated the renovation. At least it didn't prevent them from returning as soon as the last brush stroke of paint dried on the baseboards. They feel right at home. Guests hear voices when no one is there, lights turn on and off with no assistance, and apparitions are often reported.

The old hotel register is still intact, including the names of Jay Gould, J.J. Astor, and U.S. Grant. Movie director Steven Speilberg stayed in the Excelsior House once, swearing his room was haunted. He made everyone in his party get up in the wee hours and drive to a motel several miles down the highway.

During the 1870s the town was in the midst of economic woes. Their attention to the temporary financial problem became diverted by a sensational murder trial, having to do with this tale's leading character—*Diamond Bessie Moore*!

I could simply say Bessie haunts the cemetery and Excelsior Hotel in Jefferson, but you would miss out on how such a beautiful dark-haired woman with flashing gray eyes arrived there to begin with.

Bessie was born Annie Stone in Syracuse, New York. At an early age she achieved promiscuous behavior. She gave her name as Bessie Moore when traveling to Hot Springs where she became a prostitute. She met tall and handsome Abraham Rothschild, a diamond merchant and son of Meyer Rothschild of Cincinnati.

"Abe" bought Bessie everything his wealth could buy and showered diamonds upon her.

She followed him to Cincinnati then announced she was pregnant. Bessie demanded he marry her, which he said he would do, but not in Cincinnati. She agreed to go elsewhere as long as they married. They traveled all the way to Jefferson, Texas.

The glittering diamonds Bessie wore on her fingers and ears entranced the people of the town. No wonder she had the nickname of "Diamond Bessie." Of the many vices Abe may have had, beautiful women and gambling topped his list.

The day of the couple's arrival in Jefferson was sunny, but rain fell by evening. Morning brought a clear day and they decided to picnic in the woods. It is said Abe went into a restaurant where he ordered picnic lunches. They laughed and held hands as he carried the basket of food. The pair strolled across the footbridge of Big Cypress, and it would be the last time anyone saw them together.

In late afternoon, whenever anyone asked Abe about his wife, he replied she was visiting friends and he would join her later before they left Texas. Of course, when neither returned, everyone thought they had departed for the East.

For the next several days, snow fell on the small town. When it began to melt, one of the residents went searching for firewood. She discovered the body of a beautiful dark-haired young woman, a bullet in her head.

After authorities carried her into town, they agreed she was Diamond Bessie. The snow and ice had preserved her body. Citizens paid for her burial in nearby Oakwood Cemetery.

When the couple had first arrived, their luggage showed tags indicating them to be husband and wife. However, after her death, no marriage records could be found at any stop the train may have taken from Cincinnati to Texas.

All the evidence pointed to Abe Rothschild as the murderer. The sheriff traced him to Ohio, and he and a deputy left immediately to return him for trial. When they got there, they found the suspect had tried to commit suicide, succeeding only in shooting himself in the eye.

After Rothschild recovered, he was defendant in one of the most notorious Texas trials of the time. It ended in dismissal, bringing about a second trial. Four years later the jury brought in a "not guilty" verdict.

A hack waited outside the building, and before the courtroom emptied, Abe leapt into it and took the next train out of town. Many people felt certain the trial was fixed by Rothschild family money. They also speculated he left to keep from being attacked by those who thought him guilty.

Years later the cemetery caretaker's son said his father told him a handsome elderly man with an eye patch had asked for the location of Bessie's grave. He placed red roses on the site and knelt to pray. He then left, never to be seen again. Perhaps with his impaired vision, he didn't see Bessie's misty form rising to greet him.

Gravesite of Diamond Bessie Moore

Should you decide to visit the charming town of Jefferson, Texas, you have your choice of lovely old hotels in which to stay the night. People say Bessie's ghost wanders through the

Excelsior House. I suggest you reserve the elegantly furnished "Diamond Bessie Moore Suite."

...Wait, there's something glittering on the floor. Someone seems to have dropped an earring.

Revisiting Oakwood

L et's return to Jefferson and the well-kept Oakwood Cemetery where "Diamond Bessie" Moore is interred. This time we're not visiting Bessie, at least not to my knowledge. Of course, she may know we're there.

This tale came to me from someone who first heard it from his father. He wanted to see for himself, so he talked his dad into taking him out to the cemetery. Before Oakwood was fenced and gated, a person could drive inside any time the of day or night.

Blake Harris, who related the experience, said he was scared then and thinking about it now gives him an anxious twinge. One night he and his dad set out for the cemetery. As they drove down a slight incline, his father told him to look out the window toward the railroad tracks.

Not knowing what to expect, he did as he was told.

Without having anything pointed out to him, Blake saw a pair of what he said looked like "ghosts eyes" looking back at them. They seemed large and hollow—a bluish color. At first, they looked like signals on a railroad, but they were too close. Besides, a train wasn't coming or the signals would be flashing. The lights Blake saw didn't flash. They were just there, in an ominous pose.

If his dad had not been driving, Blake would have run from the cemetery in half the time.

The gate is now locked at sundown. The police keep *their* eyes on the cemetery, making it difficult for anyone to check out the anomaly.

Remember that the "ghost eyes" were there long before the area was patrolled. *They* do not belong to the police. Could Bessie possibly be looking for her murderer?

The Blue Goose

A woman named Missouri Whitehead lived in Jefferson, Georgia. Once, while visiting the seashore near Savannah in 1853, she reached down to pick up a beautiful conch shell. Her husband had died, so Missouri chose to insert the special shell into his gravestone.

Soon after, she moved to Texas to live with one of their children. In time Mrs. Whitehead passed away, and rather than return her body to Georgia for burial, her family laid her to rest in Hemphill, Texas. About 1969 her great-granddaughter flew to Georgia, planning to remove the conch shell from Mr. Whitehead's stone and embed it in Missouri's marker.

As she knelt to chisel out the shell, a most remarkable thing occurred. A large blue goose circled above and landed within a few feet of the tombstone. This somewhat startled the young woman, as it did everyone who heard about it, since no one had seen such a bird before.

As the great-granddaughter removed the shell, the bird took off in a westerly direction, soaring into the clouds.

Two days later arrangements were made to insert the conch shell into Missouri's stone. Everybody there was mystified to see the blue goose appear at Missouri's gravesite. It flew the great distance from Georgia to Texas.

Family members believed the blue goose was the spirit of Mr. Whitehead, showing the approval of transferring the conch shell, bringing closer the distance that separated them.

I first heard of this story from a cousin in Georgia. It found its way into Texas legends, as well it should, since the story ends here.

Or does it?

Indian Spirits

The Caddo Indians lived in the lush green forests of pine trees, interspersed with oak and pecan, in eastern Texas. Rivers, creeks, and clear springs provided a suitable place near which to construct their wickiups. The tribe, Hasinais, believed in the supreme god the *Caddo Ayo* for religious leadership. They prayed for the first fruits of the season and for good harvests and envisioned everyday life with the supernatural.

Many of their relatives were buried west of what is now Mt. Pleasant on Tankersley Creek. After the mid-nineteenth century, the government moved most Caddo tribes to Indian Territory.

After the Indians had left and before the white people had cleared all of the timber out of the area, a woman heard strange sounds from the bottomland's Indian burial grounds. She rushed to tell her husband what she had heard. He scoffed at the notion, but she convinced him to come with her.

They proceeded down the slope where the doubtful man heard nothing, just as he expected.

Later on two men were clearing the area and heard distinct sobbing. Thinking someone was injured, they investigated but found no one. The cries always ceased when they drew closer.

For years after, people said these sounds came from the spirits of Indians weeping over the removal of their loved ones from their traditional homeland.

Cold Gold

The truth has a way of seeping into your nerve endings. Give it a chance. This story is true. However, real names of those involved are obscured.

Mr. and Mrs. Moore lived close to an Indian burial ground reportedly located in Smith County in East Texas. For years people accepted the latter as fact.

One clear morning (with neither clouds nor thunder to foreshadow anything ominous) a woman knocked at the door of the Moores' house. Mrs. Moore answered the door to see a woman clothed in what appeared to be an Indian dress. She wore moccasins and her hair was in braids.

The woman asked for a piece of bread. That was all she wanted, a piece of bread. Mrs. Moore went to the kitchen and returned with two slices.

The visitor thanked her, hurriedly ate part of it, then looked as if she were ready to leave. She suddenly stopped and turned back. "I want to tell you something. Treasure is on your land."

Mrs. Moore thought she heard correctly. "Treasure?"

"There," the Indian woman answered, as she pointed toward the dirt road. Saying nothing, she walked down the steps and through the grass. Eating the last of the bread, she continued across the road into the field. Because the small area had long been known as an Indian burial ground, the Moores had never farmed this part of their land.

Mrs. Moore watched the woman until she disappeared. She literally vanished in a mist as she walked into the graveyard.

When Mr. Moore came home, his wife explained what had taken place, not without some apprehension in her voice. She did not doubt she had seen a ghost. They went out to the road the stranger had indicated and her husband scuffed the dirt with his boot. They had driven over that road hundreds of times. How could there be treasure under it. And what kind?

Still, the idea appealed to Mr. Moore, so he drove into town early the next morning. He and a friend returned with proper equipment since the earth was too hard for normal tools.

The task didn't turn out to be easy, and it was a hot day. About the time the men decided nothing would be found, they struck something hard. Digging out what they thought to be a rock, they were astonished to find a dirt-covered brick—a brick of gold. They reasoned the gold had been there since Civil War days. Continuing a while longer and finding nothing else, Mr. Moore decided the treasure hunt had ended.

Younger male members of the family thought they would give the hidden treasure another try. They hosed down a section of the dirt road to make the task easier. With posthole diggers and other implements, they began their work at dusk. Even water hadn't helped soften the ground. Trying to crack through the hard earth was like scraping out cement with a spoon.

They kept at it until one of the young men dropped his shovel, seemingly in pain. The other two glanced up at him but kept on working. Then one of them let out a yelp. "What's going on here? My hands are freezing."

Looking down, they observed a kind of vapor swirling upward. The young men touched the ground, quickly pulling their hands away, as if their fingers would freeze to the soil. Their exhaled breath was that of a cold January day.

They took off running. A quarter of a mile down the road, it grew warm. The warm turned to hot. It should be getting cooler as the evening went on, but it became even hotter. Gathering courage, they trekked back to the house to replace the dirt they had scrounged up in the road.

Amazingly to them, everything seemed normal once again. They packed down the soil with their shovels and went into the house. After telling of their experience, the discussion centered on the gold that had been found and gold that might still remain. For the time being, they decided not to find out, and apparently no one has tried since. They seldom talked of the story outside of family.

The gold could have belonged to Civil War soldiers who died before retrieving it. Indians could have buried the treasure. Or outlaws could have tucked it away for later—and later never came. We don't know how much gold was actually buried, but if the Indian woman wanted the Moores to have it, why did the earth turn so cold that the young men couldn't dig it up?

Like I said, the story is said to be true. We just don't know all of it.

A Mt. Pleasant Haint

This cemetery for one has its roots in the Civil War, which isn't so long ago when you think of haints as having been recognized for centuries. They may not have been called that name through the years, but a haint is a haint is a...ghost.

If a man named Hazalum (and I never learned his first name) had been a patriotic, upstanding citizen, he might never have deserved the fate that befell him. Even before the war he had not practiced the finer qualities of manhood, such as "love thy neighbor" and "thou shalt not steal." He preferred stealing everything he could.

While the boys in gray fought for their beliefs, Hazalum continued ransacking the community of Panther's Chapel, outside of Mt. Pleasant, where he lived with his wife.

Only the young and old remained behind during the war so no one could stand up to this scoundrel even if they could prove him guilty. Furthermore, he knew they could not take him.

Somewhere along the line, he hadn't counted on the war not lasting forever. When hostilities ceased and the soldiers marched home, they soon learned of the goings-on during their absence. They also knew who the suspect was, and Hazalum found out they knew. The men had fought for the Confederacy so long, they had gotten the hang of killing, so the story went. However, to kill Hazalum by hanging was not necessarily what they had planned. Using him for target practice was more to their liking.

In the meantime the cowardly thief had holed up in his house. When he realized how many men were coming after him (chances are he had been the subject of a posse before), he ran out the back door. His horse was reined at the front. He was lucky up to a point, since most small houses of the period had only one entrance and exit.

Fighting men knew how to be alert, and one of them noticed the culprit as he made a dash to the woods. They left in hot pursuit. Hazalum reportedly climbed a tree, like a 'possum being chased by a dog. Lots of trees grew in Titus County, and each one was worthy of being climbed.

It could be said that one of the men did not altogether play fair, for he raised his rifle and aimed at the trapped man nestled in a fork of the tree. How could he miss? The target had no place to go. Hazalum fell to the ground, looking for all the world to be dead. Not one man thought otherwise, even after having what they believed to be a good look at him. A circle of blood spread from his body. More blood might have seeped into the dry dirt had a neighbor not come by and seen him gasping at the base of the tree. The passerby ran home to tell Hazalum's wife. She hitched up the horse almost before the message had been completed. She reached her husband and managed to get him into the buggy. They headed in what seemed to be the safest direction—any direction away from home.

By this time someone must have observed them bouncing at a fast clip along the roadway. As soon as the men heard Hazalum still lived, they saddled their horses, gathered their rifles, and took out after him again.

Little time passed before they caught up with the couple. The unofficial posse pulled the man from the buggy with his poor wife looking on in horror. More than one shot went into Hazalum's body, this time killing him for certain and sure.

The men made a cemetery for one and dug it deep. They shoveled the dirt in on the recently departed then made themselves comfortable, waiting to see if Hazalum would dig his way out. Figuring no one could hold his breath that long, they picked up their weapons, and left.

Hazalum's wife placed a wooden marker by his grave, and it is only natural to believe it is long since gone. "Hazalum's Cemetery" was reportedly just southwest of Mt. Pleasant. That does not pinpoint a location, but cemeteries "for one" are like that.

Now we might think this story is complete. But wait.

On moonlit nights when it is just clear enough to see, there is no better place to observe haints than in East Texas. For years after Hazalum's demise, people reported seeing his haint. This was not a mysterious haze, but a form looking exactly like Hazalum running to the woods toward the big tree from which he was shot.

More than once did someone see him, and often more than one at a time, so they could vouch for each other. Interestingly, the ones who swore they saw him were mostly the men involved with his shooting.

But we all know Hazalum is dead. Or is he?

The Jacksonville Ghost

Jacksonville in Cherokee County is real East Texas, ghosts or not.

The details of this true story came from someone who has previously been a student at Lon Morris College. The haunting part of this tale is preceded by unusual occurrences in the young man's dorm.

He and his roommate dismissed sounds of doors opening and closing as simple structural problems. They also ignored the unusual sounds coming from the wall areas, especially when no one was in the room next to them.

Still, a few of these friends decided to share the same room before the rest of the students arrived. Not that they were scared....

Jason, who related this experience, pulled in a mattress from another dorm room, placed it on the floor, and *tried* to get a good night's sleep. When he closed his eyes, he envisioned a quick flash of bright light. Within the light, the number 747 became very clear. He saw nothing else. (And no picture of an airplane hung on the wall.) When he told his two roommates, they tossed it off as a dream and said no more about it.

The Jacksonville area was lush with trees and presented an invitation for exploring. Other incoming freshmen joined Jason and his friends the next night. While driving around, they discovered Pierce Chapel Cemetery. It was isolated, with no houses or streetlights—only the moon and stars. They slowed, but didn't get out of the car.

One student chose to make a return trip alone on another night, just to have a second look. Since older students had passed stories concerning apparitions and other weird happenings around the dorm, he wanted to see for himself. When the freshman went back to the dorm, a bit pale, he reported hearing footsteps crackling across the cemetery ground. He turned around but saw nothing.

In just a moment the silhouette of a person appeared, leaning against the car. The freshman called out, but the figure disappeared in a vapor. The vapor then floated upward.

A couple nights later Jason and a few of the boys drove off to Pierce Chapel. Now you can take one person's words for something or *skepticize* it away. Jason's skepticism lasted only until they arrived at the cemetery. There had been no fog that night in the entire area, and it was unseasonably dry in East Texas. Still, a low fog covered half the cemetery and never rose above the gravestones.

The boys had parked their car at the entrance. While they watched the fog dissipate, one of them called out he had seen something—a shape playing hide-and-seek among the headstones. Then another of the group spotted the "thing." All but Jason saw it. He looked everywhere they pointed, but as soon as he looked, the thing skipped ahead. At last he spotted something resembling a blue flame rising from the ground.

They watched it disappear, thinking the show was over. "Let's go," one of them said. "This is spooky."

Then the flame reappeared, moving from one grave to the other. It arose from the earth again, floating around as if taunting them. It flew to a tree where it sat on a limb, pulsating. The flame suddenly cut itself off, and the frightened boys had seen enough for one night.

When they got back into the car, the driver turned. "Jason, did you notice what road this is?"

Jason looked out the window until he could see the next FM road sign just up ahead. "747."

Later they tried to make a connection between the mysterious occurrences in their dorm, including the bright flash of three numbers and the fog and blue flame in Pierce Chapel Cemetery. They never put the events together to make sense.

Jason graduated several years ago and is now a college teacher. He still looks back on the experience with wonder, never once believing it didn't happen.

Many ghostly cemetery tales involve lights, lanterns, and spheres. However, this light resembled the shape of a candle flame. Jason says he hasn't discussed the experience much. It's one of those things he can't expect everyone to take seriously.

But we do.

A Singing Tombstone

Some people produce a melody by playing a comb. Yascha Heifetz would never have been jealous of a musical saw. But music from a stone? That would be more impossible than blood from a turnip. Well....

A singing tombstone was located on the Mathey Jackson land, a few miles off FM 1254 out of Mineola in Wood County. The land is private property and is now fenced and gated. Its gravesites probably all belonged to members of the Jackson family.

The young people of the area related tales of this tombstone many years ago. As they explained the story, the stone moaned or as some said, sang. It occupied a spot close to a stand of East Texas pine trees. This stone was the only talented marker there.

The blowing wind glanced off the top and sides of the marker, causing eerie sounds. Of course, that was only one explanation. Others say they also heard it on calm days. Speculation provides a more ghostly reason.

Curiosity seekers came for years to listen for themselves. In 1970 surveyors recorded new land boundaries. At that time all that remained were the marker's base and footstone, as the headstone had disappeared.

Could it be someone planned to take it on a concert tour?

Sugar Hill

Sugar Hill was the unofficial name given to the more or less swampy marshland of Wilkinson in northeast Texas. For many years the residents felt the name was derogatory. A few years ago they changed their minds and requested the name be officially changed from Wilkinson to Sugar Hill.

The town is in an isolated area between White Oak Creek and Sulfur River in Titus County, several miles north of Mt. Pleasant. In the late 1800s the town boasted a few stores, a gin, and a mill— the businesses a community needed.

During the years between the two World Wars, the town declined, with bootleg whiskey its chief commodity. Consequently it became known as "Sugar Hill." Some of the land appeared as treacherous overgrown forests, a perfect hideaway for moon-shiners.

Over a hundred years after its beginning, the town that once offered a newspaper to its residents had dwindled in number to less than forty. That's *living* residents. Just outside Sugar Hill is an old cemetery dating to the early 1800s.

Jade, an acquaintance of mine, told of an unnerving experience she and her husband had one warm summer afternoon. They were new to the area and decided to ride their bicycles out in the country to view the scenery. Jade had already heard stories of possible witchcraft and unsettled spirits (not the moonshining kind), but this afternoon she found her own story.

The further they rode, the denser the forest became. After riding a couple miles in the country, they came to a "T" in the road. As Dorothy's Scarecrow said, "You could go both ways."

As they were deciding which turn to select, Jade noticed an old cemetery surrounded by a fence, as well as a certain amount of overgrowth. They couldn't resist investigating and deposited their bikes outside the gate, closing it behind them.

Some of the headstones were beautiful, with others no longer legible—the mixture not being unusual.

The day was a calm seventy degrees. An eerie thing occurred soon after they entered the confines of the cemetery. By the time they reached the center, the temperature must have dropped at least ten degrees and a cool breeze had picked up considerably. Still, the sun shone bright as ever.

They thought it curious but wandered around reading epitaphs when Jade touched one of the more ornate headstones and found it to be icy cold. Stone and granite would normally be cool, even on a warm day. Touching more stones gave them the same hand-chilling feeling. They felt uneasy, as if "someone" were with them.

The couple walked back to the gates where they left their bikes. Approaching the entrance, they realized something had changed. The gates they carefully shut had swung open. Not only that, but the bikes they left facing the cemetery stood several feet away and turned in the opposite direction, toward home.

Their first instinct was someone had been there playing tricks on them. But the afternoon was very quiet with no cars on the lonely road, and the nearest house was a couple of miles distant. They had heard nothing.

The strange feeling the couple experienced that day proved enough to keep them from ever going back. For some reason the town's long-time residents whom they wanted to ask about the episode did not wish to talk about it.

Could ghosts of bootleggers have wanted the place all to themselves, making their own translucent sour mash lite?

ℌis ℜame Was Porter

ℌe fell victim to a most regrettable accident. His arm didn't make it. This time a gristmill was the perpetrator in the community of Small, in Van Zandt County. Gins and mills could always be relied on to provide injuries from minor to severe.

William Madison Porter, born in 1873, possessed more drive than much larger men did. It might be said Will Porter never believed being small in stature made him less than his peers.

According to Elvis Allen, author of *Daddy Said,* Mr. Porter maintained a variety of businesses during his lifetime, including a blacksmith shop, a syrup mill, a sawmill, and a barbershop. There is danger enough in any one of the four. A barber accidentally nicking a customer could be an introduction to a six-gun.

In the late 1800s and through the turn of the century, cotton was "King," with cotton gins thriving in small communities. The ol' boll weevil hadn't yet journeyed to upper Texas.

Mr. Porter's cotton gin was no less busy in 1906. One day he was performing the well-nigh-safe chore of cleaning lint from the machinery. We sometimes don't know how accidents happen, and Will probably didn't know how he caught his hand in a gin saw. It pulled him right through, like being on the losing end of tug o' war.

Stopping the machinery was no problem, but setting Mr. Porter free before he lapsed into unconsciousness seemed impossible to his employees. He remained awake but couldn't reach the controls to reverse the motor, and no one else knew how.

The blowing whistles brought in friends from the streets. Mr. Porter gave one of them instructions on how to back him out of the difficulty, something akin to an old-fashioned washing machine roller. Reversing the motor was the only answer.

The story goes that Mr. Porter, bleeding from face, body, and arm, didn't wish to stay around for medical help. He walked under his own steam toward his house. With mangled torso, he arrived home to await the doctors who amputated his arm right there on the front porch. Even with severe injuries, he miraculously survived and lived to his nineties.

Will's arm was buried in the older section of Small Cemetery next to his father. Will outlived his limb by many years. A family friend prepared the burial box. He took Will's arm and a hammer to nail the lid shut. This cemetery isn't really haunted as far as I've heard. Not to make light of an unfortunate situation, but...does a coffin for an arm have to fit like a glove or is it measured by standard sleeve-length?

The Performance

Christina Kidd of Houston knew as a young woman that she had psychic abilities. She was also hostess to an earthbound spirit residing in her house. The lights would go on and off and there would be no rainstorm brewing. The curling iron shut off and on and it didn't have a short.

Keys would be missing then mysteriously reappear. I often miss my keys, and they *never* reappear without my own frantic search.

One of Christina's earlier experiences concerned a beautiful and serene old cemetery about forty-five minutes north of Houston. At least it is serene during the day. Nighttime is the right time, depending on your reason for visiting.

Christina's reason? A paranormal experience, which her intuition told her she would have. A few friends did not believe in such things, so they asked if they could go along with her when next she visited this particular cemetery. "Baloney" was the word many people used.

They arrived at the cemetery before 10:00 P.M. The six of them exited the car and walked to a place Christina believed to be "home base." She directed her friends to sit on the ground and wait. Christina had seen this phenomena before and expected to again, although you can never be certain.

Perhaps a half-hour passed, during which time the others in the group grew restless.

Then "On with the show."

Bright yellow spheres streaked around an area of newer gravesites. We might wonder if this had significance—their hovering over newer graves. The cemetery itself is historical, with dates to the early 1700s.

After a while the colors grew smaller then disappeared into the blackness as if the curtain had come down on their performance. Two of the young people ran back to the car. But the show was not over.

If the two were to see the second act, they would view it from the car. The mysterious form of a lady dressed in white appeared. She moved gracefully, proceeding to stroll *through* and around the gravestones.

One might think the apparition was a misty trail left from the sphere's disappearance and had merely taken the shape of a human. But the threesome agreed the form was too precise for any old mist and was surely a woman's form. It/she continued to wander for a minute or two then dissipated as if being swallowed by the night.

Being unnerved, the other three witnesses were ready to leave. Christina accompanied them toward the car on the narrow road between the cemetery's new and old sections. They stopped suddenly. Or something stopped them.

Christina described the feeling of an enormous wall of energy squeezing their breath from them. One, however, felt nothing.

Maybe it was time to get into the car, lock the doors, and leave this place. Leave for *that* time perhaps, but Christina has returned with other witnesses to the phenomena. Not necessarily the same phenomena each time, but you wouldn't want to see the same performance repeatedly, now would you?

Sharrock's Dogs

Deep in the heart of northeast Texas lie abandoned, lost, and haunted graveyards...and oh yes, many mysterious tales of headless horsemen, apparitions, and even canines of the ghostly variety. Kaufman County has at least a few of the latter.

Kaufman, the county seat, is at the intersection of State Highways 34 and 243 and U.S. Highway 175. Originally the area was home to the Caddo, Delaware, Kickapoo, Cherokee, and Comanche Indians.

Well-known historian and cemetery preservationist Kathey Kelley Hunt and the Kaufman Historical Commission have documented the first white people who came to the area as land surveyors, one being Robert Adams Terrell. Kathey reports the Republic and Sam Houston sent them to scout the land for settlement and also to prove or disprove the tales of the Three Forks of the Trinity. They proved two forks existed—the east and west.

The county, lying between the Trinity and Sabine Rivers, retained its antebellum rural atmosphere up to 1930 when the population tripled. Prairie grasses and mesquite, pecan, oak, and elm, all known as "Texas trees," grow along the streams of the county. But more than trees make up the mystique.

Kathey has shared this spine-tingling encounter. Her particular experience took place during a recent fall visit she made to a vandalized cemetery in the eastern part of the county.

Anyone who has traipsed through graveyards on a hot day—subtropical and humid in East Texas—can find a cool drink especially tempting. Kathey stopped in the Prairieville Store for something to drink on her trip home. This was one of those country stores combined with a little café. She found a booth that allowed her a view of the television set, so she decided to sit awhile. As she anticipated watching a bit of her favorite soap opera, an elderly gentleman scooted his metal kitchen chair over to her booth.

His first words were, "You're that cemetery woman, ain't you?" He recognized her "right off" since newspapers have published her picture and written of her help in documenting old cemeteries in Kaufman County.

The man pumped her hand like a water pump and offered his first name. We'll call him Earl. He continued, saying that he bet he knew of something she didn't know.

In her preservation work, she has heard many stories while learning of desecrated or lost graveyards that need cleaning up. She never turned down possible information that would allow her to protect burial sites.

Earl proceeded to tell her that the unusual grave he knew about was one she probably never heard of. It was south, way over on the other side of Kaufman. He knew the man buried there, possibly in the only grave on his old home place.

By this time Kathey was intrigued, wondering if she really did not know about the grave.

When Earl said the man's name was Sharrock, Kathey surprised him by saying she knew of the grave and that his given name was Berry. She had seen the grave, which was a distance from the road and not likely to have been observed by passersby. She also mentioned the old house on the property.

As Kathey described the place, Earl's eyes widened the size of the apple pie sitting on the counter top. She didn't stop there but explained she had seen Mr. Sharrock's obituary in the paper, indicating he was buried on top of a hill. Since looking for gravesites is part of Kathey's Historical Commission work, she didn't find this one too difficult to locate. Earl apparently figured she would know about the hunting dogs, but he inquired to find out. She knew about them. Mr. Sharrock was known all over the country for raising hunting dogs. A dog was also engraved on the man's headstone.

Earl could have been disappointed, since he had been eager to tell her a "first," but he had not finished his tale. Leaning closer over the corner of the booth's table, he turned his head to one side then to the other

He said in a hoarse whisper, "So you heard 'em. . .when you were there, I mean . . . you heard 'em?"

And now Earl had Kathey's attention. "Heard?" she asked, not wanting to appear too interested. She had run into many a character and/or weirdo around graveyards. Still, she remained calm even though her heart probably skipped a beat during the process.

Earl was referring to Berry Sharrock's dogs! Ghost dogs bark at his gravesite, as if protecting him from harm. Now that's enough to get your attention.

Kathey admits her own eyes were bulging a little, but she listened while Earl kept talking. She felt sure he would. Earl continued by saying he and a close friend went out to the gravesite to see for themselves if the tale about the ghost dogs was true. It turned out they heard them baying, as if the moon were full. The two men cut out in a flash, never to return. They don't even talk about it to one another.

Before Kathey could speak, Earl had started on the second stanza, whispering this time so the woman behind the counter couldn't overhear. She probably wouldn't have. The soap opera had hit a climax to that week's plot, and she was obviously deeply involved.

Earl was astounded to hear Kathey had been to the gravesite by herself . . . after dark . . . by *herself*. He also knew the dogs barked only at night. The real truth was she might have been there just *before* nightfall because she hadn't heard the dogs bark. Kathey assured him she had not been spooked and that she was an ally of the dead.

Somehow this admission made Earl wince, as if frightened by the "cemetery woman." Besides, what did she mean, "ally of the dead"?

The "cemetery woman" retrieved her keys and got a refill of iced tea to take with her, then she reached to shake his hand.

He did not return the handshake but said he had to leave, too, and guided his chair back to its original spot, without ever getting up from it. It seems he may have thought there was something supernatural about this nice woman, especially if she did go spend a lot of time in old graveyards.

Kathey overheard him telling the counter lady all about the woman with whom he had just been talking. That didn't matter to her though, because she was more interested in hearing the dogs bark. She waited until evening then drove to the Sharrock place. The abandoned old house where Berry Sharrock was born in 1893 somehow still stood, although a strong wind would probably take it down.

Kathey wanted to be sure the caretaker of the old homestead knew she was there, so she parked her car where he couldn't miss it. Otherwise, caretakers have been known to bring out a shotgun to warn off trespassers. He never mentioned the barking dogs, and she wondered if he had ever heard them. If so, he possibly would not tell anyone for fear he would be accused of fantasizing.

A person would have to know the way, or the grave would never be found. Kathey knew. She climbed through the fence and could soon see Berry's grave about two hundred yards away. The moon crept up, visible from above the trees, and crickets sang as if they appreciated the cool clear night. Frogs splashed off the embankment at the end of a pool. Embankments would suffice since there were no lily pads.

Kathey walked across the causeway at the north end of the pool . . . then she heard what she had hoped for.

She knew the unmistakable sound of a hunting dog when it alarms its master of the presence of an unknown something or someone. A half-baying sound, yet somehow mournful in its warning, carried through the dense trees. The dog never showed itself, but Kathey sensed it was there. When she stopped walking, the barking also ceased. As she continued toward the gravesite, the barking began again, softer for some reason. Still a little skeptical, she wondered if the barking came from a dog chasing a night critter in the distance. But as soon as she stopped, so did the barking. The dog had to be nearby.

The moon's rays angled through the treetops, leaving a shimmering glow on Berry's granite tombstone. Kathey was too close to turn back, with less than a hundred yards to go. A rustling sound in the bushes told her something other than a squirrel was observing her. She cautiously walked closer to Berry's grave. She couldn't stop now.

The barking began—close, closer than before. The sound came from a snarled thicket about twenty feet from the grave. Where was her flashlight—certainly not with her.

The dog's incessant barking could wake the dead. Was that its intention?

They bark at night
Courtesy of Kathey Kelley Hunt

Kathey had thought to dismiss Earl's story, but now she was not so sure. All the other graveyard tales she had heard seemed to appear before her, reminding her of the doubt she once may have had. Her past efforts had been to preserve the resting places of her county's pioneers. If she ran away now, she might never accomplish her goals elsewhere.

She thought a moment, then she knew what to say. "I am your ally," she said aloud to Berry Sharrock's ghost dogs. This is similar to what we have been warned to tell ghosts. We are their friends and mean them no harm.

Kathey must have gotten her message across. The barking stopped. She walked back to the car, knowing she had her answer, at least as it concerned Berry Sharrock. She needn't worry about his grave. His ghost dogs would protect it.

The moon had dimmed. Night seemed to swallow the house, the grave, and Sharrock's dogs—at least for now.

Chapter 6

Early Texas Burial Traditions

They weren't exactly the good ol' days. Egypt possessed the art of embalming, but it would be a while before America would implement the skills. Funeral parlors had not discovered Texas in the nineteenth century, at least not in the smaller communities.

Texas law did not require death certificates until 1903 and then only if a doctor were present at the time of death. Still, he would have to report it or the death would not be documented. The deceased could certainly be buried without a record of his departure. Somehow people would know.

In genealogical research, old newspaper obituaries are treasures for specific dates. In the *old* days, obituaries of *regular* citizens were often elaborately written, as if the deceased were a state official.

Such obituaries allow us to discover what glorious lives our ancestors lived, trudging through muddy farmland, working from can to can't. Until we read their almost-biographies, we never dreamed it was an honor for great-grandmother Ellie to milk Bossy on a cold winter's morning, or place glass eggs, as if they were Fabergé, under the chickens to coax them to lay.

If the woman became widowed late in life, she continued to wear black until her own demise. Funeral services often took place in the home. Early mourning traditions varied, but dressing in black expressed the solemnity of the sorrowful period for the widow. Wearing black still denotes respect for the dead.

Black crepe was traditionally placed on the door of the deceased's family. Often the room in which the departed lay in state was draped with black or dark grays.

When a gravesite was close to the house, friends carried the departed's coffin. If a distant cemetery served as the burial site, a special wagon or hack usually delivered the coffin. The only elaborate decorations used were possible plumes on the roof. The driver might wear a stovepipe hat, even though he wore his work clothes, possibly the only clothes he owned.

After the Civil War, small buggy manufacturers produced more original designs of funeral vehicles. In larger communities, early models of horse-drawn hearses were ornate, and the driver sat high in front. Styles changed every few years until the arrival of motorized transportation after the turn of the century. However, lack of money in rural areas made the use of such elaborate transportation impractical for most people.

Even after funeral homes existed, embalming did not come into practice immediately. The deceased was laid out on a cooling board, dressed for burial, and nickels usually closed the eyelids. Later a small oval device was placed under the lids, which kept them down.

Whatever the time of death, the hours following held great importance. You couldn't wait for Uncle Dwight to arrive from Kentucky, unless a lot of ice was on hand... er, on the whole body, that is.

After embalming became prevalent, the body was prepared then often brought to the home for friends to pay their respects. The usual procedure was to remove most of the furniture in the parlor, except for a chair or two. Thus, plenty of space was available for the abundance of flowers that were sure to fill the room. This also served as an opportunity for one last photograph to be taken of the departed in his or her residence.

If a person lay for a night in a coffin in the home, someone kept vigil until morning. Before embalming, the family wanted to make sure the deceased was truly deceased. Another early belief was if a person stayed watch, an evil spirit wouldn't invade the body.

A cemetery plot would be chosen at the time of death, and if a full branching tree were available, that would be the choice location for burial.

No planned spaces were designated for plots, as in specific rows, so a necessity for some kind of marker existed. Without one, gravediggers could easily excavate another grave in an area already occupied.

Graves are still hand-dug in many smaller country cemeteries. Present-day machinery can't tell if someone is buried in a particular space and before you know it, a coffin could be shoveled up from the earth.

When a person passed on, friends often dug the grave unless a family member found it his bounded duty to do so. Those who carried the coffin would be called pallbearers today. They looped ropes beneath the coffin then lowered it into the ground. The family remained until the last shovel of earth was cast upon the site.

If a preacher were called for the service, he recited comforting words, and if he couldn't be present, a family member would bid farewell to the loved one.

The community of George's Creek in Somervell County constructed brush arbors in rapid succession since the thatched roofs would dissipate during the year. The first burial in George's Creek Cemetery took place in 1862, with a brush arbor constructed thirty years later.

In 1909 the citizens erected a tabernacle where funeral services were conducted. The closer the services were to the burial site, the better, especially in hot weather.

The George's Creek Tabernacle, like others in the state, is made with as many as fifty vertical posts, forming a square. The roof is much like that of a house, with crossbeams. Since early in the twentieth century, the roof has been shingled.

Tabernacles are open-air because in early days church services took place there in summer since it was cooler. Many such structures exist in Texas today and are used for funerals in areas in which there is no nearby church. This is an old custom that is still in use. It is traditional to have graveyard working days in many areas of Texas. Old-timers and descendants of former community residents arrive early on a given day, bringing scrumptious food. They spread it on colorful cloths on the many tables serving as permanent furniture under the protection of the tabernacle.

People visit with each other, neaten the gravesites, then share memories and food. More flowers appear during a graveyard working day than on special holidays.

Our heritage flows from one generation to another in how we live and how we die. Depending on our acculturation and religion, our beliefs differ. For years our families' traditions have led us.

Look at it this way. If your tradition is having a cup of café latte a couple times a day, you had better get going. Today is a good day to be alive.

Chapter 7

South Texas

Ghosts of Espantosa

Around 1900 a mysterious fog hovered over Espantosa Lake. It seemed sinister as it drifted along the shoreline. This natural lake is five miles northeast of Carrizo Springs, in Dimmit County. A discovery of artesian water brought new settlers to the area, which was once an old San Antonio campsite.

Travelers soon avoided the lake because of its reputation for being haunted. The Spanish word *espantosa* means "fearful." Avoiding a fearful lake makes sense.

Many legends concerning Espantosa have survived over a hundred years. The chief rumor centered on wagonloads of gold and silver being lost in its waters. Men shoved aside their apprehensions in order to discover the treasure.

If stories of alligators inhabiting the waters were true, the hunt for gold may have added a few more spirits to Espantosa. Reports of apparitions of those killed on the shores survived well into the twentieth century.

The men died where they fell, some washed into the depths and others buried in the sand, creating their own private cemeteries. There are no epitaphs, no gravestones. Were they murdered by others searching for the same gold?

Espantosa has changed. Water from the Nueces River has been diverted into the lake, and a dam and reservoir now exist. You can't walk the same shores as the murdered men.

Should you care to see for yourself if the ghostly fog still lingers, pay close attention. Does the fog shift into specter-like forms?

Or you may decide with the travelers of long ago and avoid Espantosa Lake altogether.

Casas Blancas

It is reasonable to expect ghost towns to have ghost cemeteries. However, this gravesite in Casas Blancas would be hard to find without the help of a murdered man's spirit. Casas Blancas is a ghost town seven miles west of Roma in southwestern Starr County.

This tale concerns the friction of a two-faction feud. The Garcia and Gonzales families were joined together by marriage. The Spanish government originally granted land in 1767 to Antonio Garcia. Eventually in the late 1899s, the Gonzales family obtained the land as well as the thirteen well-constructed rock houses the Garcias had built.

According to the legend decades later, the families argued, ending with the murder of one man. It is not clear why, but the Gonzaleses buried the deceased in secret in the family cemetery. The strange thing was the family left their homes soon after, in 1984, with no known trace as to their whereabouts.

It is said a ghostly apparition of the murdered man appeared one night when a family member stepped outside the house and strolled near the little graveyard. Moments later the apparition disappeared. It might be expected the rest of the family would never believe such a story until they saw it with their own eyes.

The locals attributed the family's abrupt departure to the ghost of the murdered man.

After they left, it took years for the old houses to deteriorate. By the mid-1900s only a few stones remained to mark the Gonzales land—land that is believed to be cursed. *The Handbook of Texas* tells us most of the stones were used to build new houses several miles away.

Perhaps the victim did not relocate with the old stones and new houses. It is believed he still guards his own private cemetery, the ground on which he was murdered.

Ghost Dancing

Legends are repeated so many times through the years, it becomes difficult to distinguish the "real" from myth. Of three versions I've heard about a dancing ghost, I like the one referred to by Juan Sauvageau in his book *Tales That Will Not Die*.

The location is close to Benavides in far South Texas. Once a railroad runs through a community, it becomes a hub of the area. Other small towns die away and people move into the town having the depot. It so happened with the brush country town of Benavides. Cattle were an important part of South Texas, and many trail drives that began here ended up in Dodge City and other towns in Kansas.

Our tale could be of any year as far as legends go, but as it unfolds, we learn automobiles were popular. This account appears to have taken place about 1950, and it concerns Manuel and Maria. Their names remain the same in the different versions.

Manuel made plans to attend a fiesta, although he hadn't taken time to ask a date. He didn't want to be late, so he climbed into his pickup and took off. After he had driven to within a few miles of Benavides, he was startled to see a girl standing by the road—not walking, just standing.

When he stopped to ask if she needed a ride, he was even more stunned to hear her say she wanted to go dancing. Of course, he asked her to go with him to the fiesta and she readily agreed.

Maria was not dressed in modern clothes but in a dated dress. Her beauty outshone her attire, and all the young people at the party took notice of the pretty stranger. She said she had been away for ten years and because they had grown up so, they didn't recognize each other.

Maria danced beautifully, particularly the polka, although she didn't feel secure with the newer rhythms. The party lasted long into the evening. Everyone said goodbye, and the couple strolled toward Manuel's pickup.

The temperature had changed during the festivities, and now that it was so late, it had grown quite chilly. Gentleman that he was, Manuel removed his coat and placed it around Maria's shoulders. He asked her where she lived and said he would take her home. She insisted on being let out exactly where he stopped for her earlier.

This made little sense to him, especially since her house was probably just down the little road from the highway. It might even be dangerous for Maria. However, he would grant her wish. She did agree to keep his coat since she was still cold. This suited Manuel because he had an excuse to see her again. Of course he would return for the coat the next day.

She thanked him and Manuel drove off. He looked out the window until he could no longer see her walking down the narrow road. She wasn't visible in the rearview mirror, but Manuel supposed she had already reached her home.

The following afternoon he returned to the same place and looked out over the fields. A house in the distance surely must be where Maria lived. He drove down the road and stopped.

Knocking at the door, he hoped she would answer. Instead an older woman stepped out onto the porch.

Manuel asked if he could see Maria, and the woman burst into tears. She told him her daughter had died ten years earlier.

Refusing to believe, Manuel said he had loaned Maria his coat and he knew she would expect him to return for it. If there were no Maria, where was his coat? He told the woman the girl attended the dance with him the evening before.

He then proceeded to tell her what a good dancer Maria was, particularly of the polka—better than anyone else there. Manuel even described the pink dress she wore.

The woman paled, saying they had buried her daughter in such a dress. Yet, she would prove Maria was dead. "Come, I will show you." She led the way across the road to the family cemetery. Stopping at Maria's grave, she pointed at the stone. The dates were 1920-1940. "You see, my daughter died exactly ten years ago."

Manuel's coat lay across the grave.

The tale of Manuel and Maria belongs to the dozens of "phantom hitchhiker" legends, right along with the "Traveling Nun." They can take place in any state in the country but always seem to end with the girl vanishing. She is often found out to have been dead for several years.

Milam Square

Near the western side of downtown San Antonio, you will find Milam Square—but don't look for a cemetery. It is no longer visible. The square is just north of El Mercado Street. When in the area, the first thing to remember is to keep a peaceful countenance and good thoughts.

As we have read, spirits may return because their human forms suffered violent deaths. Such is the apparent case with spirits from this old Spanish graveyard. In the 1700s Milam Square was the burial site of Spanish settlers and Indians who fought for this land.

The Apaches found their way into Texas from Arizona—not to find a new home—they were chased. The early 1880s brought the last battle between the Mescalero Apaches and the Texas Rangers. They not only fought against the rangers, but also against the Spanish people in San Antonio.

Stories say that because of the violence of these raids, people with "evil" thoughts who stroll by the area can expect to be approached by ghosts of those who lie beneath the ground. They are not your gossamer apparitions as many perceive ghosts to be, nor does their approach allow much time for an innocent bystander to leave the premises. They can be violent, the same as they once lived and died. Then they vanish, depending on your attitude—or theirs.

One version, with its beginning in the early 1900s, describes the experience of a man who saw the specters in the form of ghoulish figures looming in front of him as if to engulf him in a storm of terror. Then they disappeared. This individual harbored a personal anger at the time, and the specters sensed it.

The experiences in Milam Square continued through the years, with their stories being repeated many times. When any sort of violence occurred, such as the time in the mid-1900s when a man was in the process of robbing a pedestrian, a ghoulish specter appeared from nowhere. It reportedly grew in stature, something like a genie in a bottle, but with large black sockets for eyes and robe-covered arms reaching out. The robber lost no time in his haste to escape. The specter vanished and the relieved victim, not believing her own eyes, left the scene.

The ghosts of these early citizens rise from beneath the sidewalks on which you might be walking. They can now and then be seen in San Pedro Park close to Incarnate Word College as well as on San Saba Street. It is still best to retain an aura of friendliness.

This legend may never end, but then legends, like rings, have no end.

When walking through Milam Square, don't expect to see such specters every time, just when the spirit moves them.

The Healer

If you look closely at dusk, you might see a man's form riding a weary donkey across the wild grasses outside the town of Falfurrias. The ghost knows exactly where he is going—wherever the need is greatest.

"Tell her to cut off her head and feed it to the hogs," Don Pedrito Jaramillo told the woman who asked for a migraine remedy for her friend. The prescription might have worked as a last resort. However, this time the woman with the migraine was so enraged at the remedy, she never had another headache.

In 1880, as a young man, Don Pedrito moved from Guadalajara to South Texas and settled on the Los Olmos Ranch. He became a faith healer after curing himself of an affliction of his nose. No one seems to know what affliction, but because of the pain, he buried his face in the mud. He treated himself in this way for two or three days. Afterwards the pain disappeared.

The story goes he heard a voice from God, telling him he had the gift of healing. Believing the voice spoke truthfully, he set himself up as a faith healer. He reportedly prescribed the first thing he thought of when a person asked his help.

Don Pedrito's powers were sought for miles around. In the beginning he stayed at home, and the afflicted came to him. Many of his patients left behind their crutches after being healed.

In time he dressed as a Mexican peasant, riding to those who needed help. He never charged for his services, but the grateful gave donations, either in person or by mail. In turn he made donations to the poor and kept storerooms well stocked in order to distribute food to the needy.

Don Pedrito Jaramillo died in 1907. Most of his patients had been poor and could give only fifty cents or a dollar. After his death, more than $5,000 in fifty-cent pieces was found in his house.

Hundreds of people a year visit Don Pedrito's resting place in the old ranch cemetery near Falfurrias. A shrine is set up, and visitors light candles for the *curandero*, or faith healer.

Eliseo Torres lists many tales of Don Pedrito's prowess with remedies for illness in the book *The Faith Healer.* Another of her stories concerned a man who drank some water, not realizing a grass-burr was in it. The burr stuck in his throat. A physician told him the only solution would be to have surgery. However, Don Pedrito advised the patient to drink salt water. The man followed the latter advice and became so nauseated he spit out the burr. It is said by that time it had sprouted leaves.

People know the legend of Don Pedrito. He can be seen riding his donkey from his gravesite to the *rancheros* of those who are desperate for his help. He rides over cacti and through live oaks and mesquites. People who have not seen his ghost, light a candle and say prayers at his shrine.

Falfurrias, the land on which Don Pedrito lived and died, is at the intersection of Highway 281 and State Highway 285, south of Premont and Alice, Texas. To find the graveyard, travel east on 285 about two miles. Then turn north on FM 1418. A historical marker is at the site.

Don Pedrito Jaramillo drew people to the area in life. He draws people to the area in death.

Some say the spirit of the healer has cured them.

Chapter 8

Funerary Symbolism

After the American Revolution, stonecutters kept ledgers with their designs so families could easily choose appropriate stones for their loved ones. Symbols found on gravestones had a specific meaning.

Children's graves frequently had the figure of a lamb carved into the marker, or a small lamb statue sat next to the grave. Angels and birds also can be found on gravestones of children. Toys, Christmas trees, and balloons are still seen on children's graves.

By the Victorian era, ornamentation had reached its high point. The rich desired elaborate tombstones by which to be remembered.

Again, Europe spawned the American wish for gravestone embellishment. The symbols all had specific meanings. Many of the following are not used now as they were in the past:

- Anchor: Seafarer
- Angel: Resurrection
- Anvil: Depicts the occupation of the departed
- Bible: Cleric or religious person
- Birds: A winged soul
- Bleeding heart: Depicts Christ's suffering for our sins
- Book: Scholar or teacher
- Cherubs: Children

✧ Circle: The circle of life everlasting

✧ Cross: Symbolizes faith and resurrection. Many variances of crosses are used—Celtic, Greek, Eastern, Latin, or Russian

✧ Cross and anchor: An early Christian symbol referring to the "anchor of the soul."

✧ Doors or gate: Passing into the next life

✧ Dove: Purity

✧ Eagle, Crossed swords, bugles: Indicates that the deceased served in the military

✧ Fish: Faith

✧ Flame: Everlasting life

✧ Flowers: Life and beauty

✧ Hand with forefinger pointing upward: The deceased is in Heaven

✧ Hands praying: Signify devotion

✧ Hands outstretched: Denotes a plea for mercy

✧ Harp: Hope

✧ Heart: Love. Two joined hearts indicate a marriage

✧ Hourglass: Symbol for time

✧ Hourglass with wings: Indicates "times flies"

✧ Lamb: Always depicts innocence

✧ Masonic emblem: Marked the grave of a freemason, often used in the nineteenth century and usually found at the top of the gravestone

✧ Owl: Wisdom. Sometimes on the stone of a teacher or preacher

✧ Seashell: Life everlasting

✧ Sickle: The last harvest of death

✧ Skeleton dancing with a human shape: Dancing with death

✧ Skull and crossbones: Depicts death, often used in the eighteenth century

✧ Staff or rod: Comfort

✧ Tree: Depicts life

✧ Urn: Represents the body as a container of the soul

✧ Winged skull: Fleeting death

✧ Tree trunk: Special symbol and marker of Woodsmen of the World

Cemetery Plants and Flowers

When choosing flowers to take to a gravesite, the following may be remembered:

✧ Roses: Perfection (Remember, the scent of roses where roses are not may indicate a ghost is up and about.)
✧ Daisies: Offer hope for resurrection
✧ Rosemary: Remembrance
✧ Fern: Sorrow
✧ Lily: The Virgin's flower and symbol of purity
✧ Mandrake: Relative of the belladonna. Mandrake is believed to spring from the life forces of the interred.
✧ Iris: When clustered, the pointed blades resemble palm fronds, depicting Christ's last journey into Jerusalem.

Trees

✧ Pine trees: One of the world's oldest trees. The fallen needles deter water.
✧ Willow: Sorrow
✧ Cypress: Hope
✧ Yew tree: Represents eternal life. Commonly found in British cemeteries. However, this evergreen is in a rural Scottsville cemetery in Harrison County, Texas.

Gravesites

Many years ago grass growing over graves showed disrespect, so the families kept the soil neatly raked. A barrow or mound of dirt above a burial site kept people from walking over it.

Scraped graveyards were typically southern and can be found in all of Texas. Author Terry G. Jordan, in his book *Texas Graveyards*, quoted an old-timer as saying his father had killed himself pulling weeds, and he wasn't about to let a weed grow on his father's grave now. The scraped mounds also give a visual of a fresh burial.

One belief for using shells over a grave is that a departed mother was compared to the sea, with its waves continuing through eternity. White seashells covering her grave symbolize everlasting life. Frequently, the barrow had large shells neatly arranged in horizontal rows or in an artistic pattern.

The use of shells on burial sites is considered African in origin. In Texas an elaborate example of shell-covered gravesites is in Comfort in Kendall County. These shells have been painted or whitewashed and arranged over a concrete mound covering the graves.

Mr. Jordan quotes someone on the tradition of shattering dishes from which the dead had last eaten. "You break the dishes so that the chain will be broken and no other deaths will occur in the family."

Broken glass over the site depicted the broken life of the deceased—it also was thought to ward off evil spirits. Surely stray animals would not risk disturbing the grave.

In one cemetery in Cass County, a grave has inverted snuff bottles lined in a row in the bare earth.

Occasionally a lamp was anchored into the base of a gravestone to light the way in the journey of death. A comb or brush may have been left behind for the deceased with beautiful hair.

Superstitions or acts of love? No matter, all were respected.

Chapter 9

Coastal Texas

Do They Know Where He Is?

L iendo Plantation is an imposing ranch initially farmed about 1833. Jose Justo Liendo had first rights to the land near Hempstead in Waller County. It was later sold to Leonard W. Groce, who ordered slaves to build an impressive colonial-style house. Foundation and chimney bricks came from red clay of the Brazos. The lavish interior of the large white house included hand-painted floral ceilings, marble fireplaces, and a huge kitchen.

Who would know that long after workers completed such a wondrous home, a child would be heard crying in the night?

Upon the structure's completion, it took close to three hundred slaves to operate the plantation. According to Ed Syers in his book *Ghost Stories of Texas*, Groce helped provide for Sam Houston's men just prior to the Battle of San Jacinto.

During the Civil War, Liendo became a military camp. In 1865 it served as the campgrounds for General Custer and his soldiers. After the war the plantation met with financial disaster. In 1873 Leonard Groce had to sell the homestead for a mere ten thousand dollars to Dr. Edmund Montgomery and Elisabet Ney.

Elisabet was a spirited sculptress, born in Bavaria. She married Dr. Edmund Montgomery, a respected physician and scientist.

Because of her feminist beliefs, she didn't publicize her marriage and insisted on being called "Miss Ney."

This artistic woman sculpted European kings, as well as a bust of Prussian Prime Minister Otto von Bismarck. It was possibly due to the intrigue in which she was caught with Bismarck that she and Edmund immigrated to America, finally settling in Texas.

Reportedly their personalities did not endear them to Hempstead's citizens. "Miss Ney" continued with that name, insisting she and her husband were "best friends."

The Montgomerys named their baby son Arthur. After a historical king, perhaps? One might call his mother eccentric. As a matter of fact, many people did. It is said she dressed him in Roman clothes, similar to what she often wore. At the dawn of each new day, the young boy probably did not awaken to a joyful life, even though cherished by a doting mother. Elisabet devoted several years to rearing her son, giving up her art during that time.

Tragedy struck in the form of a South Texas diphtheria epidemic, with Arthur a victim. Despite all the care his parents could give, he succumbed to the disease. Death by diphtheria caused parents near intolerable grief as they watched their children suffer.

Edmund and Elisabet burned his body—in one of the fireplaces. After a while they removed the urn containing his ashes from the marble mantle and buried it in a small cemetery a short distance from the house.

When the plantation failed because of high mortgages, Elisabet moved to Austin and opened an art studio. She sculpted great men of frontier Texas. The Ney Museum now houses her work, including life-sized figures of Stephen F. Austin and Sam Houston. Over seventeen thousand visitors from all over the world come each year to the museum.

After Elisabet's death in 1907, Dr. Montgomery brought her remains to Liendo, where he buried her next to Arthur. Two years later Edmund sold all but the right to live in a portion of the ranch house.

It appears more than Elisabet's memorable reputation lingers nearly a century later.

From his wife's death until his own in 1911, who could know Edmund's thoughts? Did he wonder if their lives would have been better had they stayed in Europe, even though Elisabet had gained such recognition as an artist in America? Perhaps they would have been able to watch Arthur grow into manhood. Instead, Edmund and Elisabet rest next to their son in the little cemetery. Perhaps not all are resting.

The house grew old, its pillars devoid of paint. People learned from those who saw and heard, a ghost roamed through Liendo. More than once someone heard the cry of a small child, as if gasping for breath. From the effects of diphtheria? Surely not from a fire.

The house again changed hands several times, finally being restored to its previous grandeur. The mansion now sits behind a closed gate and towering trees.

The boy's ghost should be gone since his parents are by his side. Still, in the recent past, when invited guests stayed in Liendo, it was said they heard the crying voice.

Sugar Land

Hodges Bend Cemetery in Sugar Land includes resting places for veterans of wars since the 1700s. Many slender white crosses stand at their graves. Perhaps everyone interred there is not resting all the time.

As early as 1843 raw sugar mills were established. The community eventually became a town for the Imperial Sugar Company. Sugarcane, once the favored crop of the area around Fort Bend County, met its last harvest in 1928. Plant disease and federal taxes had a hand in its demise. Afterward raw sugar was imported for refining.

No other name could have been more suitable than Sugar Land. It had its lumps over the years, dissolving into a small populace and returning to a thriving community that it is today.

Nichole Dobrowolski, whose ancestors are buried in some of the county's cemeteries, has an interesting report concerning Hodges Bend. She and friends visited this cemetery one evening when the moon was full. That's the best time to visit a haunted cemetery, right? Just ask Lon Chaney Jr.

During the group's visit, they each had the urge to look over their shoulders, and they weren't looking for a bluebird. There is nothing like the feeling of being watched.

Many children are buried in Hodges Bend. One gravesite is reported to be that of a young girl named Sarah, who died in the late 1800s. A handmade metal fence surrounds her grave, giving it a delicate look of railings with corner posts on a bed. Nichole said she was drawn to the site and has visited it more than once.

Sarah's grave
Courtesy of Nichole Dobrowolski

An interesting point concerns a scent the group seemed to be aware of. They agreed it was patchouli. Scent seems too light a description for such a heavy and intense odor. But in a cemetery?

Oil made from the plant was used for preserving fabric in Indian shawls or for softening aging and cracked skin. OR for use in vaporization.

Several photographs Nichole took show ecto-mist forms in different colors, similar to those shown in human aura photography.

Note misty orbs at top of picture. Hodges Bend Cemetery.
Courtesy of Nichole Dobrowolski

When the foursome was ready to leave, the group could not unlock their car. They had to wait for help to arrive. Thank the good spirits for cell phones.

In the past people have talked of an abandoned house in the woods near the cemetery. It is not known if it has a connection with Hodges Bend, but who knows? The house had reached the falling-down stage long ago and may not be there now. Different reports told of children's voices coming from the old house, but no one lived in it.

Another tale drawing attention came from teenagers whose car broke down by the cemetery. Overgrowth at that time grew so thick the young people had to cut through it to discover the old house.

Curiosity got the best of them. They walked through the weed-choked yard to the inside of the rickety structure. They detected no sign of anyone having lived there for decades. But on their way out, they saw children's toys scattered about the yard as if someone had just played with them. The teenagers vowed the toys had not been there before.

Whatever route they took, they left the area in a hurry, their own legs carrying them.

Ye Shall See the Light

In Bailey's Prairie, near Angleton in Brazoria County, if you're in the right place at the right time—or maybe that's the wrong time—you might get a chill or two. I don't mean from winter's cold, but from the eerie ball of light. Some say the light belongs to a native North Carolinian, Brit Bailey. That's worth at least one chill.

Angleton is thirty-three miles south of Houston's County Road 521. Bailey's Prairie is five miles west of town. Brit founded this Texas location after having lived in Tennessee and Kentucky. He served a stint as a U.S. Navy captain in the War of 1812. After completing his service, he packed up his family and with their half-dozen slaves, traveled to Texas. They settled on the banks of the Brazos, land that later became Brazoria County.

Stephen F. Austin accepted Brit Bailey as one of the "Old Three Hundred," the first families who received Austin's "Impresario Contract." This allowed them to take possession of a headright of over 4,000 acres of land at a bargain price.

It seemed to suit Brit Bailey just fine. A controversial figure when leaving Kentucky, he continued his reputation in Texas. He came close to losing his land when Mexico regained its independence from Spain, but Austin recognized his squatter's claim to land near what is now known as Bailey's Prairie.

Even though Bailey survived various battles and gained a name for himself in the military, he also became known for his eccentricities and his penchant for brawling. The man apparently loved a good fight—or even a bad fight.

Records show he died of cholera in December of 1832. However, a modern-day autopsy might have found liver disease the real cause of his death. If a caption underlined his portrait, it could well read "Brit Bailey, lover of the whiskey jug."

Being a creature of detail, Bailey's will stated specifically that he desired to be buried "facing west" in a standing position so he could continue walking in the after-life. He wanted his rifle by his side. He apparently didn't ask it in his will, but he wanted a whiskey jug at his feet. Not an empty jug—it had to be filled with whiskey, of course.

His desires might have been carried out, except his wife's wishes took precedence. His wife Nancy was the sister of his first spouse, Edith Smith. When it came to the question of the whiskey jug, it is said Nancy refused to allow it. It was high time he remained sober. The jug did not accompany Brit to the great bar-room in the sky. He would probably have drunk its contents before he got that far anyway.

First the man, now the ghost. As early as 1850 reports of weird lights hovering around in Bailey's Prairie attracted everyone's attention. People saw a vertical light swaying from one place to another, much like someone walking and carrying a lantern.

Animals acted strangely when the light began to glow. With the advent of the automobile, it is said the cars sometimes stopped as if the key fell from the ignition.

Often the light appeared in the shape of a single ball, floating from four to six feet above ground. It is safe to say that in the early nineteenth century, Texans knew nothing of electromagnetic energy, as in orb. Follow the ball's movements and it looks as if it is searching, searching. No need to ask for what. The whiskey jug of course. Could Bailey's light be Bailey's ghost? Or is that how rumors get started?

In 1970 the Texas Historical Commission placed a marker near Bailey's land to commemorate his life.

According to *Ghosts Along the Brazos*, written by Catherine Munson Foster, who purchased Bailey's Prairie, the light appears during the fall—at night. She also wrote that it hasn't been seen as much as in the past, maybe only every seven years.

Has Brit given up the search? Perhaps he has been on the wagon so long he has been cured of his drinking habits (not exactly cold turkey since he has been searching over a century for his whiskey). He may just sit down and rest during the off years.

As yet I haven't observed Bailey's Light, but seven years from now. . . .

Postscript: Author Catherine Munson Foster is buried in the private gated Munson family cemetery. It is located off Highway 35 near Angleton and next to Bailey's Prairie. Reports indicate it is not necessary to enter the cemetery in order to see a light from within. It is apparently not from a house, but . . . just what does Brit Bailey's ghost do during those other six years?

Down Under

As far as anyone knows, the hundred-year-old Alief Cemetery in Harris County had no reason to be less than peaceful until the late twentieth century.

At an earlier time Alief, a present residential suburb of Houston, was called Dairy. Different people purchased and sold the land after it was first settled in 1861. One man, Francis I. Meston, purchased the farmland in 1893. After applying for a post office two years later, the town changed its name to Alief, after the first postmistress.

At the turn of the century, Mr. Meston gave land for the cemetery. However, the town suffered heavy damage from a flood in 1899 and from Galveston's hurricane the following year. Residents left and the town once again became a prairie.

Relief came to Alief when its former residents returned a few years later and rebuilt the town. Businesses prospered. Through the first half of the twentieth century, the town had its ups and downs, and in the 1970s Houston annexed much of the community. With so much disturbance to the land, how could any residents of Alief Cemetery be contented? No wonder they wander.

The suburb of Alief is southwest of the city, near Dairy Ashford and Bellaire Boulevard, with the cemetery located where those streets intersect.

The paranormal incidents did not occur until developers planned apartment complexes in that area. It is said part of the plan was rejected because no survey showed the exact boundaries of the graveyard. Still, it seems apparent that a portion of Alief Cemetery was down under a section of an apartment unit.

Talk about unrest. More than once there have been reports concerning weird happenings in a few of the apartments. Poltergeists do indeed provide weird happenings. The word comes from the German language. Though commonly translated as "noisy ghost," actually *polter* means "to knock" and *geist*, "spirit." Therefore, poltergeists sort of knocked around the house, as in tossing vases across the room and tipping over coffee cups. Who turned off the lamp when someone tried to read? People have moved out of their residences for such frisky intrusions.

A poltergeist can throw a real scare into a person when the poor ghostly thing may be only mischievous.

Nevertheless, the people who live in the apartments near or "over" Alief Cemetery do not take kindly to poltergeist activity, especially when they are uninvited.

Mission Espiritu Santo

Perhaps the legend of the nun is true—then perhaps none of it is. You be the judge.

The Mission Espiritu Santo was founded in 1722 near Matagorda Bay. In the mid-1700s the mission was relocated to its present site on the northeastern bank of the San Antonio River near Goliad. The rich green pastures were perfect grazing lands. At one time a herd of 40,000 cattle roamed on this land. Cattle supported the mission and led to the development of Texas ranching. Every day cattle were butchered and distributed to the thirty-three families that once lived there.

Espiritu Santo served as a mission for over a century, with its nuns constantly busying themselves with their sacred duties.

Over time the buildings were redesigned and used for public school facilities. It was one of the first educational institutions serving Spanish-speaking Texans. The mission went through several troubling times, including disrepair. The site of the mission was donated to the state in 1931 and transferred to the State Parks Board, later to be the Parks and Wildlife Department.

It was partially restored in the 1930s and includes a granary, church, and a workshop.

Today the area is a state park, a beautiful spot for tourists. It includes a museum, campgrounds, and a nature trail. The park has over 72,000 visitors a year. This does not include the non-earthly visitors who have been reported. It is estimated twenty or more people were buried in the mission compound around the stone church, which dates from 1777.

Some people have seen a white-shrouded woman gliding through the site. It is best that her shroud is of wool, since she seems to appear when the nights are chilly. Was the ghostly lady in white looking for a loved one who died, or does she play the role of a caretaker of the mission?

It is said a little nun will be seen in one place in the church, vanish, then quickly reappear somewhere else. Perhaps the nun was interred in a graveyard by the stone church. As a spirit, she feels the need to tend to her former duties. She has been seen by different observers, none of whom doubted the nun's *habit* of mysterious appearances.

Tears in the Night

Chipita Rodriguez, believed to have been the daughter of Pedro Rodriguez, fled with her father from Antonio Lopez de Santa Anna. They located in San Patricio de Hibernia, Texas. She was quite young, which would make the date in the early 1800s. She was reportedly in her sixties at her death in 1863.

Many tales have been told of the first woman to be legally executed in Texas. Her gravesite beneath the tree that took her life can no longer be located. Some say lightning struck it down soon after Chipita was hanged. Legend says it did not take long for her to die. Perhaps the white flowers of the mesquite were blooming, even in November, the month of her death.

After Pedro Rodriguez died, Chipita found herself impoverished. There was not timber suitable for building log cabins. The people built houses by digging trenches into which they stood small tree trunks for walls. Thatch served as roofs. During this time the young woman managed to make a bare living by serving meals to travelers. She allowed them a night's sleep on a cot on the shanty's porch.

Chipita made a wrong decision in her choice of a man who stopped by her little house one night and decided to stay a while. Some time after she bore him a son, he saw no need to stay longer. He left, taking the boy with him, breaking Chipita's heart.

Years later a traveler named John Savage stopped for food and a night's rest. He carried several hundred dollars' worth of gold in his saddlebags. At some point from the time he stopped at Chipita's, he disappeared. His body turned up in a burlap bag in the Aransas River. He had been murdered with an ax, and the townsfolk accused Chipita of the deed. The intriguing thing was, his gold lay nearby.

Could a slightly built woman, no longer young, have managed to put a burly man's body in a bag and carry him to the river? If he were already at the river when murdered, Chipita would still have had to stuff him in the bag. Even if she managed that and if she killed him for his gold, why leave it behind? No help from fingerprints. They weren't used in the United States until 1882.

Her accusers believed she did not commit the act alone. Another person who had just come into town, a young man named Juan Silvera, was accused along with her. According to one legend, Chipita recognized him as her son, as only a mother could, even after many years.

Records tell us the courts indicted both of them on circumstantial evidence before District Court Judge Benjamin F. Neal. One tale says Juan escaped, but Chipita went to trial, never intimating he was responsible because she believed him to be her son.

A poorly selected jury including questionable characters convicted her. She maintained her innocence with her only words being "not guilty." Even though the jury asked for mercy, Judge Neal ordered her to die by hanging.

Another version reported Juan, as her accomplice, received five years in prison. Upon his release he left the area in a hurry. A wise move if this version is true.

Some people believed Chipita did not kill John Savage, but their voices were not loud enough to be heard. While being held at the sheriff's house until the execution could be carried out, two lynching attempts failed. Eventually the death wagon transported her to the mesquite tree from which she would hang until dead on November 13, 1863. A mesquite would suffice—long slender branches—strong enough to hold the weight of a frail woman.

Occasionally someone as white as the ghost he has just seen says Chipita was weeping down by the riverbank. Others say she is a specter with a noose around her neck, crying. Many have seen her, especially when a woman is in danger.

Records show that in 1985, state senator Carlos Truan of Corpus Christi asked the Texas legislature to absolve Chipita Rodriguez of murder. Governor Mark White signed the resolution on June 13 the same year.

No one knows the complete story of Chipita Rodriguez and her son. Did her ghost appear, crying for him or protesting her innocence?

As long as people remember the legend of Chipita, her spirit lives.

Protective Orbs

If Brit Bailey's "light" isn't enough to be cautious of in Brazoria County, Jamison Cemetery is something to reckon with.

Bailey, a veteran of the War of 1812, and his wife and six children arrived in southwestern part of the county in 1818. He then gained title to over forty-five hundred acres of rich land. A town sprouted around his plantation, with much of the remaining area taken up by several large family ranches. As the little town grew, so did the cemetery plots.

Nichole Dobrowolski credits Cathy Nash of the Brazoria County Cemetery Preservation Committee with rediscovering Jamison Cemetery. On Nichole's first visit there, the two women struck out in rubber boots, through twisted trees and waist-high weeds, until they arrived at the cemetery. Boots are essential when trudging through weeds—snakes, you know.

A concrete wall about four feet high and with a metal horizontal railing on top surrounds the cemetery. Concrete steps are provided for walking up and over. We would hope cattle had not figured out this maneuver. Whoever constructed such a wall seemed determined to keep the cemetery protected.

Even though the name indicates a private family cemetery, many gravesites occupy the area. There is a children's corner in one portion. Most old cemeteries have numerous tiny graves because of various epidemics taking lives of babies and children in the early days.

Just outside the wall, you can see sunken areas indicating graves. They have no markers other than a few broken pieces of rock serving as puzzle pieces for brief inscriptions. The interred could have been non-family members, and their own families preferred them to be buried close to a cemetery if they couldn't be inside. It seems plausible they could have been sites for slaves of the period.

If, on a scorching South Texas hundred-degree day, you can feel a constant "cold" breeze inside the wall, then something paranormal is taking place. This apparently isn't a one-time occurrence, since it has applied itself to several people on different occasions. The coldest spot seems to be in the children's section.

Shadows of faces and full vaporous figures are seen where nothing is there to cast a shadow. As for the moving orbs, as they develop, their size increases. They seem to give off energy, quite easily felt by whoever is in their way. As night begins to fall, the energy becomes more pronounced, almost engulfing the visitor.

Stones are inscribed with Victorian epitaphs and symbols of the time. The cemetery isn't large, but one would think the orbs are protecting it. It is very old, with birth dates from the 1700s.

No wonder the Jamison spirits are protective. Theirs is an exclusive *home* behind the wall.

An exclusive home for several spirits
Courtesy of Nichole Dobrowolski

Bigger Than a Briar Patch

The Big Thicket by any other name is still a dense forest. This tale involves the area of woods near Saratoga, Texas, in Hardin County. To clarify the location, the dirt road from Bragg to Saratoga is your destination.

That is the where—now for the what.

The "Saratoga Light" is the attraction and can be seen only after dark. For some reason a fall night is good for your adventure, perhaps because it is closer to Halloween and all things scary seem more frightening then. But don't rule out spring or summer—just go at night.

Thick piney woods loom in front of you, seemingly impenetrable. You may think twice before getting out of your car. With windows rolled down, one can hear frogs in the distance, communicating with other frogs or whomever or *whatever* might be listening. Crickets chirp while you wait for a banshee to scream, although none has ever been reported in these woods.

Normally, during a still night with stars flickering in the sky, a person sitting in a car would have only a slight degree of uneasiness. Since the light has never been explained and trees tightly hug each side of the road, could the light not come from behind and engulf the car? So far nothing so drastic has taken place—only frightening tales of a dancing, swerving light, much like a lantern.

It is said the Saratoga Light in the Big Thicket begins as one small glimmer of brightness then grows, often to the size of a basketball. If a man is on foot and sees it, the light can see him and will give chase. But if you give chase first, it will disappear, sometimes like the evasive action of a shooting star into the trees.

For decades the light has drawn curiosity seekers. They brought with them an element of danger inasmuch as a few people came armed. Someone carrying a light in order to see a ghost carrying a light, could be shot.

That was the what—now for the *who*.

Railroad tracks were laid at Bragg Road in 1904, providing the area's timber and oil resources for a rail link. They were taken up in the 1930s, with the remaining land being used as a well-traveled road. After their removal the Saratoga Light became prominent. The railroad was important to the area, as it was to all small towns at that time.

Many tales have been told about the light and who it is, or whose ghost it is, or whose ghost is carrying it. A twentieth-century justification said faraway automobile headlights flashed through tiny separations of tree limbs. That has been discounted through rational and scientific explanations.

One account explains the light as a piece of remaining ember when Confederate soldiers tried to burn out Jayhawkers who wouldn't fight for the South. This version adds a spark to the story.

Another local tale is a railroad worker's wife ran away with a lumberjack, and the husband never heard from his wife again. After the broken-hearted man died, his spirit roamed the forest and still carries his railroad lantern, looking for his faithless wife and her lover.

OR the light comes from a lantern the ghost of a railroad worker carries. He had the misfortune of being killed by the train, and his ghost is trying to signal the train to stop.

When people reported seeing the light, they disagreed as to its size and color. It is said the color ranges from yellow, to flame, to pumpkin. A pigment of their imagination?

A tale most suitable for this book concerns the railroad and the Mexican cemetery. Mexicans were hired to help cut the right-of-way and lay tracks. According to the story, the laborers were not paid by the day or week. The foreman announced he would keep their pay in reserve until the work was completed, then give them their accumulated wages.

The legend states that rather than give them their money when they finished, he killed them all and of course kept the money for himself. It may be the foreman had an accomplice, for the workers were buried in a hurry in the dense woods.

The troubled and unsettled spirits of the dead Mexican workers are said to haunt the land that caused their deaths. In misty lights, they wander from place to place within the woods, looking for the foreman. That could answer the question why the light seems to disappear in one spot then reappear in another.

Should you visit the Big Thicket, you might want to brush up on your Spanish.

According to records, past county commissioners wanted to sell the timber bordering Bragg Road in order to add to the economy of the county. Residents would have none of the idea. They liked the dense foliage that added to the mystique of the legend.

Through the years people have had varying ideas as to the source of the ghost light, and nonbelievers are in the majority—

until they see for themselves. No one can say with certainty the reason behind the phenomenon. One thing is sure, the ghostly light appears periodically at night, and most people who have encountered it are quick to say they do not choose to do so again.

Think on this: If you decide to venture down Bragg Road with its thick canopy of trees forming an overhead tunnel—you just might see the light.

Beneath the Land

Graveyards have been virtually covered up throughout Texas. Over time, this cover of earth, dust, and weeds shields old graves from sight. If it were not for original documentation, all signs of their existence would be lost, except for family history.

A family may have buried Grampa Lucas, Gramma, and three young victims of an influenza epidemic beneath the shade of a crabapple tree by the barn. Everyone knew that. Years later the barn fell apart, the crabapple tree died, lightning struck the house, and the family moved away, leaving the ashes of their homestead of a hundred years. But who would remember the family cemetery?

Housing developments and even towns may have sprung up over these old resting places. If glasses fly out of kitchen cabinets and televisions lose power, a poltergeist may be trying to capture your attention. At least it found its way from confinement beneath the house. How firm a foundation? Or shake, rattle, and take its toll.

Some lost and some found cemeteries in the Fort Bend County area seem to lap over others. Even though many seem to be well kept, cemetery names are not always known.

A man named Schendel founded this particular southeast Texas community in 1891 and thought of calling it Schendelville, but for a joke, he changed it to Needmore. It needed more at the time, for sure. Since another town had already latched onto that name, the post office changed it to Needville.

The picture shown with this story is of a cemetery close to Williams School Road and Foster Road. The photographer shot the photo on a partly cloudy day with thunder and lightning in the distance.

The transparent orb in the lower part of the picture is especially clear for daylight hours. You can see right through it.

Large orb at lower center
Courtesy of Nichole Dobrowolski

By the way, has anyone ever heard from Grampa Lucas? I hear he was a thin man.

The Tale of a Dog

Throughout history the phenomena of large black dogs have appeared in folklore and legends. In general, they have fiery red eyes. It is said they appear without warning and may even walk along with a person then disappear in a flash.

People have reported seeing dogs dash across the road and appear to be hit, but no sign of the dogs remain. Don't try to talk people out of believing their dead dogs have reappeared, curling up on the foot of the bed. They *believe*.

One phantom dog tale takes place in far South Texas, near the center of the Lower Rio Grande Valley, often referred to as "The Magic Valley."

The city of San Benito is bordered on the west by Mexico and the Gulf of Mexico to the east. San Benito is rich with Mexican culture, and its beauty draws many tourists to its recreational areas. Palm trees and tropical plants add to the luxurious terrain. This city founded in 1904 is on U.S. Highway 77/83 five miles south of Harlingen.

Several old graveyards are located around San Benito. Two neighboring ones are on a stretch of backroad behind this town. We find our story there.

The legend concerns a dead dog that has been struck by a car. When the next driver comes along, the natural thing for him to do is try to avoid running over the animal. As he swerves, the "mangled" dog rises to its feet and chases the car. If a person walked along the highway at night, the creature would rise in a crouch, then chase the pedestrian. The person walking would gasp for breath, knowing he had already seen the big circle of blood on the road. How could the dog come alive?

It is believed by some that the dog is guarding the cemetery as phantom dogs often do. But the sighting is also accompanied by a green light appearing to come from the caretaker's cabin.

The person who related this tale to me has spoken with several people who claim to have witnessed the tale of the dog.

But the dog's tale isn't as important as the dog!

A Traveling Nun

Many of the stories in this book may sound familiar, just enough like those you've heard before to make you think they're the same. For instance, many versions exist of the story of poor Chipita, the woman who may have been wrongly hanged in San Patricio.

This story involves a nun who seemed to gain frequent flyer miles as a ghost.

The first time I heard an intriguing story of a traveling nun was twenty years ago. A friend of mine who now lives in North Texas once told me about a nun she and her husband picked up on the outskirts of El Paso on I-10. The nun didn't say much during the drive but blessed them for stopping on such a warm day. She insisted on being let off at the roadside on the way to Fabens and she would walk the remaining two miles or so.

Thinking that her walking might have been an atonement of some kind, they agreed. Later they wondered if the sister really existed.

According to folklorist Ruth Dodson, in *The Best of Texas Folk and Folklore*, a nun had made several appearances. More than once someone picked up a nun along the roadway and let her off in a small town. It turned out no one in the town had even caught a glimpse of the sister, much less heard of one in the area. There was no convent, not even a Catholic church. In 1945, with sisters wearing long black habits, surely someone would have noticed.

Another of Dodson's legends reports a man was driving along the highway in South Texas, on his way to work for the W.P.A. A nun walking on the gravel shoulder of the road hailed the driver, who stopped for her. After they conversed for a while, he told the nun where he worked. She said she also worked for the W.P.A. office in Alice. She asked if he would come back by and pick her up, and of course he agreed. After telling him her name and where she would meet him later in the afternoon, she got out of the car.

The man finished the day's work and drove to the address. When he arrived, she was not there, nor had anyone heard of her.

He was curious about why the woman would have given false information. Thinking she may have met with foul play, the man drove to the convent. To his surprise, the sister told him a nun by the same name had died a few years before.

In another tale, similar to the last, a nun was again given a ride by two men in South Texas. Before arriving at the town, she requested they let her out at the Catholic cemetery on the town's outskirts. They asked if they could come back for her, but she said no. They watched her enter the cemetery and disappear from view. The land was flat with no trees. Nothing could have shielded her from their sight.

Doubting their own sensitivity in letting the nun out with no transportation on such a hot afternoon, they drove into town to locate a priest.

The priest couldn't imagine who she would be. The men told him her name, and recognition appeared on his face. At that point he brought out a book of photographs.

They easily identified the nun by her picture.

The priest then told them, "She has been dead for several years."

Yet another version tells of a nun getting on a bus at Goliad. That surely makes sense because the Mission Espiritu Santo was located there. The time is in the early days of World War II.

Servicemen on the bus thought nothing of the friendly nun conversing with them. They considered it unusual when she told them the war would be over before year's end. Many people had hoped it would be true, but how would the sister know?

After the travelers relaxed a bit, one of them noticed the nun was no longer on the bus. It had not made a stop since she boarded. Where had she gone? And her luggage?

Still, a few of the men and the concerned driver continued to their destination and stopped at the convent the nun had mentioned. The sisters were not expecting anyone that day and specifically not a nun.

The servicemen seemed so persistent, the sisters showed them photographs of sisters who had previously served there. The look the sisters directed at each other indicated this might not be the first time such an incident had occurred.

The men recognized one photograph as his passenger. With stunned expressions, they heard a sister say, "She has been dead...for several years."

Now before you decide none such nun-ghosts exist, would an entire bus full of servicemen believe someone they had conversed with existed only in their minds?

Poppet's Way

It doesn't really matter whose way. The fact is something or someone got in the way of a Newport subdivision being developed in Crosby, Texas, back in the 1970s. But the underlying factor is a burial ground.

When the Purcell Corporation purchased this land in Harris County for residential development, crude wooden crosses still stood from the days of slavery. The original owner deeded some of the land to former slaves for burial of family members.

It is said the corporation, not aware of the partly fenced graveyard, bulldozed the wooden crosses and proceeded to build over the land.

Do you recognize a forthcoming ghostly tale? Of course you do. If you read the book *The Black Hope Horror* by Ben and Jean Williams, you are already familiar with it.

This young couple lived in the Deer Park area. Ben worked at the Ethyl Corporation, a large chemical plant. When his wife developed respiratory allergies connected with air pollution in Deer Park, they looked for another place to live.

The Newport neighborhood, still close to Ben's work seemed far enough away from the chemical plant. From the first day they looked at the area, with its many trees and country atmosphere, they liked what they saw. Purchasing a lot on a street named Poppet's Way, they put together their house plans. Trees often need to be moved from a lot before a house is built, but one giant oak tree on the Williams' land caught Jean's attention. She wanted that tree to stand just outside her living room windows.

Funny thing about the tree. An arrow with a couple of other markings were carved into its trunk. Whether any significance could be directed at the arrow wasn't known then. Even now it can be only speculated. Possibly young teenagers pledged their love. It happens. Nevertheless, the carving appeared to be very old.

The couple built their house and began their dream. A bad dream. They were the first to build on the east end of Poppet's Way.

From the beginning, Ben and Jean reported mysterious and puzzling things occurring inside their home. For years builders have sprayed houses for termites and other insects before the buyers ever moved in. Chances are the Williams family had this done. If so, it seemed not to have any effect on the flying critters that tormented them.

Imagine running from thousands of flying, swarming black insects. Once that ordeal was over, think about the snakes slithering about the yard.

Although the graveyard was not a large one, the Williams' house apparently was built on at least a part of it. Several rectangular sinkholes appeared in their backyard. When the builders leveled the lot for home construction and grass was planted and watered, one could easily interpret the low places as gravesites.

The Williams' garage doors opened by themselves and pet birds died for no explainable reason. The couple began seeing black forms following them inside their *dream* house.

Ben and Jean Williams' grown daughter died under mysterious circumstances. She was in remission from a serious illness, but the cause of death was a massive heart attack, possibly being brought on by fright. This tragedy continued the family's deterioration, both in health and in spirit.

Other residents also reported strange happenings. While excavating for a swimming pool, a neighbor unearthed bodies in the backyard.

Ben and Jane had no choice. They moved out of state. They had been so traumatized by the events from the time they first moved to their house on Poppet's Way, they wrote a book about their experiences.

There is more to this mystery. Pete and Carolyn Haviland, founders of Lone Star Spirits Paranormal Investigations, headed an investigation of the area in 2000. When the group arrived where the Williamses had lived, they walked toward the woods across from the house. Once they were within the wooded area, two misty black forms appeared—the same kind Ben Williams had earlier rushed *through* to protect his wife.

According to Mr. Haviland's reports from their last investigation, several similar black forms encircled the group at sunset.

By the time cameras were ready, the shapes ducked out of sight, as if knowing someone would be photographing them. Ghostly images usually do not pose for photographs. One camera malfunctioned. This is not unusual during paranormal experiences. The same is true with flashlights and certain types of recorders—not always, but frequently they fail.

Mr. Haviland relates this further intriguing revelation of their evening on Poppet's Way. During the investigation, he made eye contact with one of the dark shapes. His first sensation was a tightening in his stomach then a numbing cold all over. As if that were not enough, he then felt a stunning pain in his neck, like being hit on the head with a two-by-four.

With tears of pain, he backed out of the woods. His partner, Katie, verified the experience.

Katie Phillips told me this was one of their earlier investigations. She was an affirmed skeptic of the Williams' story, but she was eager to see for herself. She and her husband Dean, who was also skeptical, became even more so after the group told him he stood less than ten feet from one of the shadowy shapes and hadn't even seen it. But on the third trip, he became a true believer.

According to his wife, he saw two of the forms and stared them down. These Lone Star Spirits investigators know what they saw and what they observed on the east end of Poppet's Way "was not of this earth." Katie says none of them doubt the Williams' story now.

As this story is being written, very little paranormal activity is reported in homes on Poppet's Way. Several houses remain vacant, however. Occasionally police have received false alarms, showing nothing but appliances such as television sets turning on and off. I have one of those eccentric sets, but I know it's an electrical short. Whether spirits or short circuits, there is no denying the Williams family experienced horrendous trauma on Poppet's Way.

> "I believe our souls belong to God."
> ~ Jean Williams

A Jealous Sister

Stafford, Texas, is one of those small towns in the fast-growing Fort Bend County. To be specific, it is on Farm Road 1092 and the boundary between Fort Bend and Harris Counties.

William Stafford founded this community in 1830, early enough for Antonio Lopez de Santa Anna and his troops to stop at the Stafford plantation on their way to Harrisburg. They stuffed themselves on everything edible before ordering the plantation's buildings to be burned. So much for gratitude.

That tale is only a little scary and has not much to do with ghosts, although I have heard Santa Anna later may have had a difficult time crossing over. That's crossing over from one life to another—not the border.

The tale begins with information given me by Nichole Dobrowolski, whose great-great-grandmother was buried in Stafford's Craven-Ellis Cemetery. She immigrated to America in the mid-1800s. The sad part of the story is that she died at the early age of twenty-nine, leaving seven children.

Craven-Ellis Cemetery
Courtesy of Nichole Dobrowolski

It is said her vindictive sister beat her severely then pushed her off a bridge in Sugar Land, Texas. Yes, that would tend to have tragic results. The fact that she was pregnant with her eighth child made it a double murder.

Family knowledge indicated it was impossible for the sister to contain her jealousy, but they did not say why she was jealous. Nevertheless, she committed murder. It couldn't have been she wanted more children than her sister had, because she had done fairly well herself, having mothered a brood of her own.

She too died at an early age. Even though her death was attributed to influenza, family members seemed to refute that reason. At least the story handed down indicated as much, so the real cause of death is apparently not known.

The sister was buried in an isolated spot in Craven-Ellis, not in the usual "family corner" as they used to say.

Her husband remarried soon after her death, a common practice when small children were involved. This family moved to the Blessing-Palacios area to start a new life.

Nichole says she and family often visit the cemetery; she feels affection toward her murdered ancestor. A photographer, Nichole has taken several pictures in the cemetery, many showing ectoplasm mists and orbs. In some cases the orbs are like vertical spheres, standing close to her or even following by her side as she walks.

Ecto mist at top and orb in lower corner
Courtesy of Nichole Dobrowolski

At certain places in the cemetery, sudden strong breezes gust through particular trees, as if someone is controlling the movement. On several of her visits she recorded the unexpected whirlwind noises, almost hurricane-like. The sound was much stronger on the tapes than when she heard them in person.

Could this be the action of her great-great-grandmother to be lovingly recognized, or is it the ghost of the sister who cannot rest?

Another brief tale has emerged within the last fifteen years concerning a teenage boy. It seems he would sleepwalk to Craven-Ellis Cemetery. He slept among the tall weeds, and his parents would find him the following morning. The boy died young and was buried close to where he sometimes slept.

It is said he may have foreseen his own death. This seems to carry dress rehearsals a little far. Did a voice direct him there to sleep or was it true sleepwalking?

The cemetery at one time appeared abandoned because of the overgrowth. It is now mowed on a regular basis. As I mentioned earlier, a graveyard need not be old to have ghostly apparitions, although this one is.

Knights and Daughters

Carolyn Haviland, a founder of Lone Star Spirits Paranormal Investigations, shares an experience in Knights and Daughters Cemetery in Houston.

She and other members of Lone Star Spirits chose a chilly evening to visit the cemetery, so Carolyn wore a jacket the entire time. Wearing the jacket turned out to be important.

From the moment they first entered the graveyard, Carolyn felt they were being watched. That is not an unusual feeling for such a place, but this seemed different. Carolyn felt *really* watched.

She was last in the group, a space she would gladly relinquish on future investigations.

Dense brush and trees formed a backdrop for Knights and Daughters Cemetery. Weed-covered broken gravestones made a perfect obstacle to trip over if they didn't watch their step.

The cemetery extended farther than expected, and the more they walked, the more gravesites they detected. Graves in the back of the cemetery seemed to cry for attention—even a little T.L.C. would help.

Other than the eerie atmosphere of the place and the temperature changes, the group had a pleasant enough stroll through a cold, dark, ominous, and spooky graveyard.

The truly bizarre part of the tale is yet to come. After returning home, at some point toward early morning, Carolyn's back began to sting. She asked her husband Pete to check for insect bites, which seemed unlikely since she had no obvious bites elsewhere.

He was stunned to see scratches covering her right shoulder. Carolyn said it looked as if someone had scraped their nails several times on her back. Red welts were obvious.

The fact she wore a heavy jacket prevented tree limbs or thorn-covered vines from piercing her clothes. Besides, her jacket was not torn and she did not remember such an incident—an easy thing to remember.

Pete's comments about the cemetery were equally disturbing. He said an extreme cold came over him. This was backed up by the EMF readings on their equipment. (An EMF detector is used to provide authentic evidence of paranormal activity.) His right arm became numb, and he heard faint voices. The feeling of being unwelcome was overwhelming.

After thinking it over, Carolyn came to the conclusion that whatever presence lurked in the cemetery that night, it did not appreciate their wandering around in its final resting place. Either that or the presence wanted to attract the group's attention in a big way.

Remember Goliad

It is said ghosts appear when their human forms have been violently killed. Such may be the case with the massacre of Colonel James W. Fannin and his men in Goliad in 1836.

Now this story needs a bit of background history. Goliad was the original name of Presidio La Bahia, which served as one of the most important Spanish settlements in Texas. Soon after Mexico gained independence, the name was changed. Its strategic location during the Texas Revolution made it desirable, being sought after by Mexicans as well as Texians.

That is a reason our subjects, Colonel Fannin and his men, found themselves in the midst of the Battle of Coleto Creek.

General Santa Anna crossed the Rio Grande to put an end to the Texian rebellion and ordered General Jose Urrea's forces to recapture La Bahia from the Texians.

Fannin had already abandoned La Bahia, but Urrea tracked him and his men a few miles out. His forces were too strong for the Texians. After a fearful battle, over three hundred Fannin troops surrendered on March 20, 1836.

Fannin understood the law as meaning his men would be treated as prisoners of war. Had he not believed that, he may have had second thoughts about surrendering.

General Antonio Lopez de Santa Anna looked at the law differently, overruling the agreement. He ordered the entire force to be shot to death on Palm Sunday, March 27. Fannin and his troops suffered violent deaths. Their bodies being stripped and left unburied emphasized the dishonorable execution.

The event presented the largest loss of life in the cause of Texas Independence. When the dust had settled, General Thomas Rusk and his men gathered the remains and gave them a military funeral. "Remember Goliad" became the battle cry at San Jacinto.

The Presidio La Bahia is now a national Historic Landmark, one of the world's finest examples of a Spanish frontier fort. Goliad

State Historical Park, on which the Fannin Memorial monument stands, is located one block southeast of Presidio La Bahia. Over 72,000 people a year visit this park near the intersection of U.S. Highway 183 and 59.

Legend says Fannin and his men roam their burial sites, not accepting death. Colonel Fannin, as leader of his troops, may still be searching for General Santa Anna in order to have a fair fight. If he had to die, he would do so honorably.

If you are one of the thousands of visitors this year, and if you see Colonel Fannin's ghost, you might give him this message. Not only did Santa Anna fail at San Jacinto three weeks after they put Fannin to death, he later lost a leg in battle. Even though he succeeded militarily for the most part, he died poor and blind in 1876.

Perhaps Colonel Fannin should order his men at ease. They deserve an eternity of peace.

Wagons in the Mist

Something about Brazoria County provides us with scary cemeteries. Nothing jumps out and says "Boo!" but the atmosphere will get you if you don't watch out.

Many soldiers of the Meir Expedition, the Texas Revolution, and the Civil War are interred in Sandy Point Cemetery. It is on land once belonging to a sugar and cotton plantation. If you don't cotton to the eerie mists and orbs, this one is not for you. That isn't to say you can actually *see* apparition-like mists with the naked eye.

Sandy Point is a large old graveyard occupying private property for so many years, growth is thick and giant oak trees cast their shadows until no one pays attention.

The people who lived on the property knew the graveyard was there but didn't offer to talk about it unless someone asked.

Nichole Dobrowolski gave credit to Cathy Nash of the Brazoria County Cemetery Preservation Committee for discovering the long-lost graveyard. She studied maps of where it was known to be at one time then took it from there and located it. The cemetery probably became lost when the main road that used to run beside it was redirected. In time cattle knocked over and broke gravestones. That's a major reason why many small family graveyards and even large country cemeteries are surrounded by fences.

The mausoleum, once occupied by Benjamin F. Terry of Terry's Texas Rangers, is in disrepair; but preparations for its refurbishing are underway. Terry's remains were moved to Houston after he received recognition as a war hero.

The cemetery is eclectic in appearance, with flat and above-ground headstones, tall monuments, individually fenced family plots, and some smaller graves with more delicate wire protection.

Even if the day or evening is still and otherwise warm, a strong breeze filters through the trees. Normal or mysterious?

Boy Scout troops as well as inmates of the nearby prison helped the Preservation Committee rid the cemetery of weeds and overgrowth. Before the cemetery was cleaned up, it would have been impossible to see from the road, but now it is not so difficult.

Earlier pictures taken of the graveyard by Cathy Nash showed thick ectoplasm energy. After the cemetery was cleaned, Nichole's later photos still indicated mist, but not so heavy. Can it be the spirits found it easier to breathe? The cemetery is lovely now. Any spirit should like being there.

Not everyone anticipates a cold spot brushing against an arm or face, nor does everyone have the same sensation of fear when visiting a cemetery late at night. When a friend accompanied me to a cemetery discussed in this book, she had the premonition something ominous was about to happen. We left before I could get my camera focused. Of course her premonition could have been because a big green pickup followed us all the way from the cut-off to the country cemetery.

The point is, and I think there is one, a skeptic might not admit a cold spot is a cold spot when the weather is hot. Someone with an open mind can suddenly be aware of temperature change or feel something or someone, other than the man in the moon, is watching.

Decades ago sounds of horses and wagons were prominent on the cemetery road. People say they can still hear horses' hooves and rambling wagons stop and start, as if letting someone off by the cemetery.

Sandy Point Cemetery can make the hair on your arms stand up during a late-night visit. I hear you will be aware of something there that will cast aside your doubts of ghosts. Don't go alone, even without a green pickup following you.

Chapter 10

Coffins and Caskets

And Away We Go

The first Texas coffin was probably no coffin at all. A pine box came next. It was made to conform to the person's body shape: narrow at the feet and broad at the shoulders. Daniel Boone reportedly "tried on" his burial container to make sure it was the correct size. Walk right in and ask for a 42-Long.

In some state death records, coffin size was listed with the rest of the burial information. A genealogy buff could at least determine the approximate size of an ancestor.

A local carpenter would build a pine box and call it a coffin. He often made it a comfortable fit for the deceased, like 6'8" x 2'2" and 1'9" deep. The builder received few complaints.

Livery stables and general stores once offered a supply of coffins, but an individual was frequently called upon to stop what he was doing and put together a pine box.

After 1900, furniture stores in small towns carried an assortment of coffins, right along with their tables and chairs. An enterprising individual could search out a town with no funeral home and thus find himself a thriving business to operate. No license required.

A container or coffin with an escape hatch was actually put to use in Texas, but it was first patented in Europe in 1868, making its inventor wealthy. The coffin was designed so that a cord was placed in the hand of the assumed deceased. "Assumed," since it was sometimes difficult in those days to know if a person was truly dead or only in a coma. The cord extended through the lid of the coffin then attached to a bell. Should the "corpse" awaken, he had merely to ring the bell, sounding the alarm. Someone stayed on the alert for as much as a day to listen for a possible signal.

In some cases, for whatever reason people had for opening a coffin, fingernail scratches were found on the underside of the lid. That was reason enough for the invention of an easy escape route.

In one of actor Ray Milland's later pictures, the plot concerned such a theme. His character made sure the cord and bell in his casket were installed correctly. The problem? Someone cut the cord.

The inventor of the above patented casket was said to have burned himself to death to make sure he was not buried alive.

As written in Penny Colman's book *Corpses, Coffins, and Crypts*, metal coffins of the mid-1800s conformed to the human shape. A glass window at the head allowed the face to be visible.

People used coffins for different reasons. How could there be more than one? In early times one variety had a false bottom. A rented coffin provided an impressive look to carry the deceased to the burial site. After a few words were spoken over the grave and the coffin was lowered into the ground, someone flipped a mechanism, letting the bottom drop. The body would be released and the container could be used again. Recycling had to start sometime.

Up until the 1700s, the first colonists were buried without coffins. When no coffin was readily available and a quick burial was necessary, they dug the grave deep.

Did less wood make for a cheaper coffin? In the 1890s to supplement income as a farmer, my great-great-grandfather Hawkins built pine boxes for two dollars each.

In those early days of the Old West, business fairly boomed. The communities still had no funeral homes, since embalming had not yet become the practice.

DeCamp Consolidated Glass Casket Company in Muskogee, Oklahoma, manufactured solid glass coffins in the late 1800s. They reportedly did not survive through the nineteenth century.

By definition, a coffin was a wedge-shaped receptacle for a corpse. By the early twentieth century, a different style came into use, called a casket. It was a rectangular box, made with various woods, sometimes decorously carved and stained. People of means often designed their own caskets of hand-carved woods. Early linings were made of cotton or muslin. As years passed, quilted satin came into use and is still the trend. Personally, I would like a Hawaiian hibiscus pattern.

An interesting ascent or descent, as the case may be, into the next world took place during Civil War times. In Jefferson, Texas, everyone knew how much a certain couple of men despised one another. Becoming engaged in a personal battle, each man reportedly ended up dead at the other's feet. They were buried in the same coffin, perhaps left to settle their differences in the afterlife.

Laurie Moseley of Parker County, Texas, wrote an interesting story in one of his newspaper columns. It concerned the "Cantrell women," Martha and Kate, leaders of a cattle rustling gang. They were sometimes called by the name of "Hill." Perhaps no one knew their correct name.

This gang was one of the worst in northwest Texas. The law tracked them, located a suitable tree, and hanged the pair, leaving them to swing in their respective nooses.

Eventually the Texas Rangers picked up the women's bones and put them in a dry good store's box—by that time the bones had dried good. According to Mr. Moseley, the men also buried the women's long hair that had fallen from their heads. The box may not have been an ideal coffin, but by social standards, it beat a Brown Mule Tobacco Box.

The rangers buried the women under a tree in a Springtown cemetery. They tied the rope on a limb over the site as a marker for a rustlers' grave.

Martha and Kate apparently decided not to enter the paranormal world, "swingers" though they had been. No sightings have been reported of ghostly women jumping rope in Springtown Cemetery.

According to Carol Rust's article "Buried in Texas," millionaire oil heiress Sandra Ilene West selected her own burial transit:

Her 1964 Ferrari. Sandra could afford the crane it required to lift her and the car then lower them into the burial site. Cement trucks and a construction crew helped carry out her wishes.

Prearranged plans required the driver's seat of her powder blue Ferrari to be adjusted to a preferred degree of comfort. She selected a favorite lace negligee as her going-away ensemble. Her will stipulated she would not leave a penny of her inheritance if the instructions were not carried out to her specific wishes. How would she know? However, all was done according to plan, and Sandra West's grave is parked in the Alamo Masonic Lodge Cemetery in San Antonio.

Taxi, Anyone?

The National Museum of Funeral History in Houston displays unusual burial containers from all over the world. They include a giant wooden crab, a black and white cow for a child's coffin, a giant parrot, a fish, and an eagle.

An interesting story accompanies a coffin built for three, on display at the museum. A couple's son died and the parents were so distraught they decided the husband would kill his wife then commit suicide. They ordered the unusual coffin made for three.

Before they carried out the scheme, they possibly received counseling, because they canceled the order. The coffin had already been made, so they donated it to the museum.

The Fisherman

A gentle East Texas man, who was aware he would die soon from a malignant brain tumor, knew what he wanted to do before leaving this world. His doctor had given him four weeks to live.

This fisherman would forge his own casket out of iron, in the shape of a fishing boat. He had long been a craftsman, so constructing his casket would not be a difficult task. Steve needed only a little help from a couple of friends to carry out his wish.

After completing the major work, he formed handles of iron in the shape of small anchors. At the close of his service, he wanted the anchors to be removed and given to family members. According to his wishes, his wife painted the casket watermelon red and green. A friend painted a scenic design on the underside of the lid—a lake setting with clear water and tall trees shading the shore.

Steve kept his sense of humor. When he and his friends finished the project, he told them they had better watch out. "Somebody is going to want to order one." When he could joke, he did.

He outlived the doctor's prediction by two or three weeks. I'd like to think of Steve donning his waders and stepping out with his rod and reel into the clear water of that scenic lake pictured on the lid of his coffin. After he spends time there, he would find a cool rippling stream and catch many speckled trout... no catch limit.

The message here seems to be if you want to choose the mode of transportation you prefer for your final send-off, make it known ahead of time. Assuming you have a one-way ticket to ever-ever land, accept that comfortable satin pillow you are offered.

Bon voyage and have a good trip, y'hear?

Chapter 11

West Texas

The Vigilant Wife

The cattle industry had begun its full swing, and the railroads were welcomed in West Texas in the late 1800s. All this activity helped establish a community called Baird, named after the director of the Texas and Pacific Railway, Matthew Baird. That seems equitable.

Many people who migrated to Texas and traveled through the town liked it so well they put down roots. One might say that during the period from 1884 to about 1910, it took considerable strength on their part not to transplant. A fire in 1884 and a tornado in 1895 interfered with progress. Then a man named Vargas swung from a noose for murdering Emma Blakeley—a legal execution.

Wait, another disaster occurred the first decade of the next century. A runaway train reportedly caused a sensational three-locomotive pile-up at the Baird depot. Still, the population grew for several years.

The unusual part of this tale concerns one couple who decided to stay around Baird in the early days.

You've heard "There's not a jealous bone in her body," but what about "There's not a jealous body on her bones"?

No one seems to know what kind of relationship the woman had with her husband in Baird. The wife apparently kept a close rein on her spouse in life as well as in death. It is said after he died, his wife roamed the graveyard at night, seeing that no one got close to her husband. Anyone who saw her didn't linger when she chased after them.

Whatever the cause of the woman's death, she did not relinquish her guard duty over her dear husband's grave. Through the years people have reported seeing her spirit carry a lantern, keeping an everlasting vigil.

Don't venture too near

It is said she can be seen in the old Baird Cemetery. About twenty miles east of Abilene in Callahan County, exit north where I-20 intersects Highway 283.

Oh yes, once you see the Vigilant Wife, please don't venture too close to her husband's grave. She might come after you, too.

Stella

S"tella had a last name, but perhaps it doesn't matter now. You see, she is a ghost and has a right to her privacy. However, if she's looking for sympathy, we could say, "Poor Stella. It should never have happened."

We will never know the reason the lady in question had for not allowing the oilfield men to drill on her land. The fact is they wanted to and she refused.

This tale takes place during the 1920s and 1930s when oil was becoming an important commodity in Hutchinson County. Back in those days, an independent wildcatter with a couple of helpers could drill a well wherever he thought they might strike oil.

Phillips Petroleum Company constructed its first plant in the Panhandle in 1927. Stella owned land on Spring Creek that flows from Carson County into the Canadian River.

As the story goes, a few men, perhaps wildcatters, drank from the whiskey jug and reached the inebriation point. They approached Stella one last time, telling her they wanted to drill for oil on her land.

We can visualize one scenario. They stepped up on her front porch and knocked on the door. "For the last time, will you let us drill on your land? We know there's oil there!"

And Stella refused... for the last time.

They dragged her out of the house and looked for a tree suitable for hanging. They didn't need a large one for a woman. The murderers finished their deed and left Stella swaying from the noose.

Eventually friends discovered her body. They cut her down and buried her on her own land. The rope swung from the tree for many years after, until it fell apart.

It is said Stella roams about, protecting her property from trespassers. Many people say they have seen her ghost. They didn't say if she was running off any wildcatters, past or present.

Thurber

Haunted cemetery or not, Thurber is a ghost town with a history not matched by many towns its size. Stop by and visualize what used to be and now is not, midway between Fort Worth and Abilene on Interstate 20.

Coal-mining operations began in this place about 1886. After the Texas and Pacific Coal Company bought out the business, the town made a name for itself and became the most important coal mine site in Texas for thirty years. It had the best-equipped brick plant west of the Mississippi. Many important streets in the state are paved with Thurber bricks, including Camp Bowie and Main Street in Fort Worth. The old Swift and Armour plant in the stockyards has Thurber bricks lining its walls.

The town became the only thoroughly unionized town in the world. But of course the miners kept striking. It's true that the vast amount of coal opened the door to the great Southwest. But about 1917 when locomotives turned to using oil, the coal helped close Thurber's doors. More than 125 million tons of coal is reported still unmined beneath the ground of Thurber.

The town once had a population of up to 10,000 people, with over 1,000 being buried in its cemetery. Half the sites are of children. Nearly 700 graves are unmarked, but most of those are identified with white metal crosses or white plastic pipes.

The cemetery has three sections: African-American, white Protestant, and Catholic, each with a separate entrance gate. In one section a man is buried next to two adjacent and identical

White crosses among the bluebonnets (Note the distant smokestack)

gravestones, one for each of his wives. Guess a man never can be too careful in not showing partiality.

A gentleman who at one time lived in the area tells the intriguing story about a resident of the cemetery, Anthony Bascilli. An eight-foot wooden cross marks the man's grave. He dug it himself and lined it with Thurber bricks, then marked it with a cross. Mr. Bascilli was concerned about the hasty shoveling of dirt after his departure. He spread the word that he had hidden several bottles of whiskey in the soil that would be used to cover his coffin. Now that would ensure a bit of caution to his friends who would want to retrieve undamaged spirits.

Bascilli also placed a new suit and shoes at the foot of his coffin. Not only that, a metal door was hinged over the casket, dirt shoveled in, then another metal door with a lock over the casket. Then a key was dropped down a pipe into the casket. Apparently, the man wanted a sure way out on Resurrection Day.

The land had so many rocks buried beneath the surface that when digging a grave, dynamite had to be used in one section to blast out the earth. A woman might be washing dishes in her kitchen some distance away and hear dynamite explode. The sound was as good as a party line, except for her not knowing who died.

Now that the visual of Thurber Cemetery is presented, where are the ghosts? Apparently, no one has reported seeing Mr. Bascilli roaming through the cemetery. That may mean the key trick didn't work.

Thurber has long been called a ghost town. *Dallas Morning News* columnist Frank X. Tolbert once wrote that only eight residents were on the census of 1980. The popular Smokestack Restaurant, formerly known as The Ghost Town Café, is situated north of I-20, next to the smokestack. The New York Hill Restaurant, a favorite steak and seafood restaurant, is on a hill south of I-20.

The proprietor during the 1980s of the former said he had lost three employees because of the ghost sightings. That's one ghost, but more than one sighting. According to sane and reliable sources, a beautiful female dressed in white appeared on Thurber streets, singing arias from Italian operas. She disappeared before completing them.

Hundreds of Italian miners, along with other Europeans, came to Thurber to help work the coal mines. Join that with the fact the town boasted a fine opera house, and we have reason for an Italian operatic diva. The Thurber Opera House was an important stop for opera companies traveling across the country.

According to Mr. Tolbert, a resident of Thurber spoke with Eliza Whitehead, who had seen the ghost in 1955. Mrs. Whitehead was walking downtown one evening. "…And here comes this pretty young lady singing in some foreign language. Then she just vanished in front of my eyes."

Others have also reported seeing the singing ghost. My informant told me of a convincing theory a gentleman now in his nineties had on the ghost lady's possible origin. When he was about ten years old, around 1920 when the town boomed with 10,000 people, he and some of his buddies would meet at the ballpark on top of Graveyard Hill, next to the cemetery. They would play "kick the can" and other games of the times. They just might have smoked a little cedar when no one was looking.

One night when they decided it was time to go home, they noticed a lady dressed in white, sitting on the top step of a stile at the southeast corner of the cemetery. She appeared to be crying or praying in a loud voice, perhaps for some loved one buried in the cemetery. The kids didn't say anything but avoided the lady and hurried home. The next evening they returned to their regular meeting place. When they left they followed their regular route, not thinking the lady would be there again. To their shock, there she sat. They were really scared this time and took off running.

They talked a lot about the experience during the next few weeks before gaining the courage to return to the hill. Nothing occurred out of the ordinary on the way, but on their return? The lady in white started toward them. Panic prevailed and the boys ran, breathless, all the way home. They never wanted to go back to the ballpark to play.

Soon after this last incident, the citizens moved the park to the east side of town.

Thurber was abandoned about 1935 and became a valid ghost town. Since then sightings have been late at night in the downtown area and *former* downtown area. None have been reported recently.

Other theories of the singing diva: After a performance, she was late and her opera company left without her...or, she eventually died, perhaps to return to finish her career as a singing spirit...or, maybe the opera singer passed on, occupying one of the 700 unmarked gravesites, stepping out for one last encore. Perhaps the crying and loud praying the boys heard was actually singing? Few ten-year-olds would recognize operatic arias.

Some say the singing is merely the wind whistling around the smokestack or through the old buildings. Eliza Whitehead would never believe that. She heard the singing ghost with her own ears.

The Right Wind's Telling

Abandoned graveyards are not all haunted, but no one likes to be forgotten, including spiritual beings. It's no wonder Plemons Cemetery in Hutchinson County teems with sounds and eerie happenings from more than one source.

The town was named after Barney Plemons, son of state legislator William Buford Plemons. During the first decade of the twentieth century, it looked as if the community would grow into a "real" town. It even had a string band, and you can't say that about every place this small.

As often occurred during that time period, the Rock Island line bypassed the town, going through Stinnett, which became the county seat. After staying around for another twenty years, the citizens of Plemons finally gave it up. They deserted the town and moved to neighboring communities.

Naturally the residents of Plemons Cemetery stayed behind. Several children were also buried there, even though many markers are gone.

The terrain in the area is flat, with mesquite, cactus, and prairie grasses. The land is sandy, which may or may not be the cause of graves having been easily moved. Now who would move graves in an old cemetery? It isn't as though more space were needed.

Still, the dead and their coffins have reportedly been moved. Low places could be from mysterious excavations, the chasms being partially filled with blowing sands of the Panhandle.

Since no caretaker has been there for years, the graveyard fell victim to vandals. The people concerned about the cemetery's upkeep discovered signs of devil worshiping; they placed a fence made of metal-welded pipe around the graveyard. No one proved the cult responsible for moving the graves, so who *did* move the coffins?

The devil worshipers allegedly continued to meet under the bridge on a nearby road. The road is now private and inaccessible to the public.

But the tale is not yet finished. Even before the town moved, people reported hearing children's voices in the cemetery. On occasions it seemed as if they were almost fighting. Could the sounds have come from the wind blowing through the mesquite trees? Most disregard that theory.

If the voices truly are those of ghost children, the night winds will not tell.

Balmorhea

Twilight releases imprisoned shadows in this windswept graveyard of West Texas. Weaving shades of history of such a place will help form the tale.

In the early times Indian and Mexican settlers farmed the area. Abundant water came from nearby San Solomon Springs, but the town of Balmorhea was not laid out until 1906. The syllables in its name were derived from surnames of the three founders, Balcom, Moore, and Rhea. Fair enough. Apparently, they didn't want to flip a coin.

The location of this town of less than a thousand people is on Toyah Creek, Farm Road 1215, and U.S. Highway 290, just southwest of Brogado in southwestern Reeves County.

Visualize a "boot hill" kind of burial site, such as western movies offer. This gives you a picture of Balmorhea Cemetery. It's lonely out there; at least it would seem so to visitors. We can't speak for the ghosts who reside in its caliche, rocky soil.

No vegetation grows, which does not explain why locusts and other insects survive. They appear to communicate with each other when folks come to pay respects to their loved ones or to attend funerals through the years. Leaving flowers on a gravesite offers beauty that otherwise is not present, except for three poplar trees citizens have planted. If shadows appear, they come from something other than the trees.

Terry Patrick, who lives in the area, told me the feeling that creeps over her has never changed during the times she has attended family burials. Even while driving down the poorly marked, dark country roads toward isolated Balmorhea Cemetery, she anticipates the feeling, always with anxiety.

A person can be buried in this cemetery sans coffin. That is true. If the burial takes place within twenty-four hours of death, a shroud and a six-foot chasm are the only requirements. Shrouded in sheets like "Casper the Friendly Ghost" would be legal.

One section of the cemetery is for whites and the other for Mexicans, with the feet of the latter facing south to their homeland of Mexico.

Many members of the same families are buried there, with dates going far back into the nineteenth century. Descendants place flags at sites on appropriate holidays, and an uncle in Terry's family has hand-dug graves many years for relatives and friends.

Terry says she is not the only one to hear strange sounds— whispered conversations seemingly emanating from beneath her feet. Locusts may burrow in holes in the ground, but this is not the humming she hears.

The "hardy" stock of folks in the area know of the sounds. They visit the graveyard and simply accept the whispering as a kind of phenomena. They also experience a chilling sensation throughout the area.

The causes of death of those interred in Balmorhea may be the answer. Several victims of the tornado that destroyed Saragosa in 1987 are buried there. Other victims of tragic deaths rest—we hope they rest—in this land.

On one occasion Terry heard a child's distinct laughter, and another whispered in reply. She was bewildered because no children had accompanied her and other adults on that day. However, a relative showed Terry a small plot, telling her it may have the answer. It was a double grave with a stone wall surrounding it.

Years before, a distraught mother became drunk at a local bar and drove herself and her two little daughters off a mountain road. The children were killed, but the mother lived and later moved away.

The father began constructing the stone wall immediately following the funeral. For several nights after working late into the evening, he was found asleep on their graves the following mornings. This continued until he completed the wall. Even today, toys and notes can be found on the grave, after twenty years.

Hallowed though Balmorhea may be, it is surely haunted ground.

That Was No Lady, That Was My Strife

Many legends have been told about the Lady of the Lake. The best-known tale is of her presentation to King Arthur of his magical sword, Excalibur. But wait, this tale is not about *that* lady. If it were, the magical powers she learned from Merlin would have saved her.

The dictionary defines a legend as an unverified popular story handed down from earlier times. This tale has many versions, much like the game young people play, "I've got a secret." Each person relates it differently.

Lake Fort Phantom Hill near the abandoned fort's ruins in Taylor County is the location of the tale. Soldiers of the new Fort Phantom, established in the 1850s, protected early settlers in the Abilene area. Some said the fort, ten miles north of Abilene, became haunted after it was abandoned at the outset of the Civil War. Among the ruins are the stone commissary, a guardhouse, and a few tall chimneys.

The latest version of our story tells of a beautiful young woman and her beau who planned to meet at the lake, an idyllic spot for sweethearts.

When he arrived he accused her of a not-so-nice rumor. Apparently he believed none of her explanations of the truth and consequently held her under the water until she drowned. So where was Merlin when she needed him?

We don't know whether or not the young man was remorseful or if anyone ever heard from him again.

The lady is said to stroll the lake area, searching for her murderer. She carries the same lantern she lit while first waiting for her lover. Every now and then someone vows to have seen her ghost dressed in the same white dress she wore when drowned.

Another version had her fiancé not showing up for his wedding. Heartbroken and in tears, she couldn't imagine anything less than a tragedy having befallen him.

Searchers later found him dead in a small boat on the lake, with no indication of what he was doing there in his wedding attire or how he died. The Lady of the Lake roams the shores, still in her wedding dress, looking for her groom's killer.

The initial version of the tale possibly took place during that time in the late 1870s when the last Comanche Indians were forced to move on.

The young couple set up housekeeping in a wooded location—choosing to build a cabin—perhaps not wisely, in the near-midst of the Plains Indians Territory.

Legend says the husband, becoming quite aware of the danger involved, told his wife not to open the door to anyone but him. He would address her so she would know who was there.

For a time their plan never failed. Then on one occasion while he was out hunting, Indians ambushed him. He ran for the safety of his little house in the woods, banging on the door trying to break through, only to be greeted by a fatal rifle blast from his wife. He didn't give the password.

Later, after the poor woman died, she was destined to search for her husband's soul whom she felt she murdered. Sometimes she is seen gliding, as if on air, across the waters of Lake Fort Phantom Hill.

Which version do you believe?

You might see her, but you must follow specific instructions. On three consecutive nights, drive to Phantom Hill Cemetery near the old fort. Wait one hour and two minutes. Timing is said to be important. The young woman's ghost should appear, carrying a lantern and surrounded by a misty haze.

Searching for her husband's soul, she wanders through the gravestones—a loving wife who killed her husband.

You will know her from the haunted look in her eyes.

The Anson Light

According to many who have witnessed the Anson Light northeast of Abilene, there is more to it than merely a tourist attraction.

For years in Anson, the headlights reflecting on tombstones in its cemetery have remained a popular theory for the Anson light. Other people prefer a more mysterious explanation, which draws sightseers by the cars full.

The town of Anson, county seat of Jones County, has a population of approximately 2,650. Originally called Jones City, Anson was first established at Fort Phantom Hill. With the anticipation of a railroad going through a nearby site, the town was moved. However, the railroad never developed. Jones City was renamed Anson, after the last president of the Republic of Texas.

The ghostly tale of a grieving mother surfaced perhaps a century ago. It is said the woman's little girl became lost in a snowstorm, only later to be found frozen. Another version says that the child was murdered. Legend has it the mother searches for her daughter every night, carrying a lantern—an accepted source of the Anson light.

On warm summer nights people drive for miles to see the phenomenon. Some reports indicate when the light appears for the first time it is blue, then red, growing larger as it soars into the trees or hovers above a gravestone.

If the mother's spirit is carrying her lantern, she can very well fly around if she wants. Someone has even said the light appeared to take on a near-human form. You may question that if you wish.

Karla McKinney DeCluette, a former college student in Abilene, tells of some friends' experience with the mysterious light. They had driven their van to the area and while they were parked close to the graveyard, a strange red dot floated their direction, growing in size as it came nearer.

A bizarre thing then occurred. The van began to shake. The motor refused to turn over, as if possessed by the light. On the third try, the key connected and the young people sped away.

When Karla heard the story, she and other students elected to see for themselves. Their experience was much the same.

A ball of light landed on the hood of the car and skittered into flight like a shooting star. Such a sight would shake up any onlooker, van or not. This was not the case with Karla. *They* shook, but the car did not . . . It took three tries to start their vehicle.

Karla does not live in Abilene now. However, she may return for a college reunion—she just might not stop by Anson Cemetery.

What *is* the light? Could it be the headlight of the train that never materialized, looking for the tracks that never were? Television's *Unsolved Mysteries* investigated, returning a "no decision" verdict. Or perhaps it really is the grieving mother's lantern.

Why not have a look for yourself? And while you are in the area, go by Lake Fort Phantom and wave to the young bride in her wedding dress.

Anson Revisited

Returning to a site that provided a paranormal activity the first time can make your nerves jiggle. Would it be the same the second time around? We have already been to Anson through the eyes of others, but this time we are going with Aimee Wilson and some of her friends.

The group rode in two cars. Nine people needed two cars. Aimee gives us a glow-by-glow description of their experience. They left just before midnight on one night in February. Driving down the road next to the cemetery, the first car stopped on top of the crossing to wait for the second to arrive. Both cars parked side by side, facing the cemetery.

Some people say the best way to see the Anson light is to flash your car lights three times, as if knocking on a door. One version of the legend is that two boys went into town on an errand for their mother. She told them if they ran into trouble to flash their light three times and she would come help them. So if a car's headlights flash three times, the Anson light is said to be their mother responding.

Both groups flashed their headlights, then waited about five minutes. The light appeared, disappeared, then returned. It moved up and down, side to side, never the same pattern.

Aimee's seven-year-old son said he thought "she," meaning the light, was pretty. He wanted to see her again and in a minute or so, *she* reappeared. The second car's driver decided to move the car toward the light. The boy was afraid they would make the lady leave so they stopped the car and the light remained very bright.

At that point the two cars drove forward. The light disappeared. The procedure seems almost like stepping on the mat of an automatic door and it opens and closes if the person moves back and forth.

When the driver of the first car got out and walked toward the second, Aimee thought his car was moving backwards. She wondered if she was seeing things. They talked about that a moment then decided they had seen enough for this visit and decided to leave.

The light had gone out of sight by then. But as soon as the first car started to leave, the light returned. Aimee's group watched it a moment, then it floated back into the cemetery. Perhaps the woman had given up and realized her sons were not coming home this night.

The next evening the friends all got together and discussed the experience. An interesting point is that when Aimee felt the other car was rolling, an occupant of that vehicle also felt the car was rolling backwards. As a matter of fact, she had that sensation the entire time they were parked. "Like something didn't want us there."

Everyone came to the conclusion that if the light was indeed a spirit, it was a friendly one. The next time they venture to Anson Cemetery, they are going to time the light intervals to see if that can determine anything else.

Just because a major television show found no answer does not mean there is none. If you have visited this place, you may have another version—other interpretations of what you viewed.

Whether the light comes from a mother looking for her frozen child or a mother searching for her two sons, the fact remains, people from all over the state and beyond go to Anson to see the mysterious light for themselves.

Crying Dog

Kimberly Olsen, an active member of the El Paso Chapter of Southwest Paranormal Investigators, related this story, one her grandmother had told her many years ago.

It concerns the Mission Trail Cemetery near San Marcial in El Paso County. To reach it, take I-10 from El Paso, south past Socorro about twenty-five miles. The cemetery is on the old mission trail southwest of El Paso. There are several tiny "two-horse" hamlets down there in the old farm country around the river.

Abandoned farmhouses and neglected cemeteries add to the atmosphere.

Kimberly's grandmother, a spiritual lady whose house nestled in the Franklin Mountains, told the story many times through the years to the children. It was the kind of tale children sat still to listen to.

Over seventy years ago, when the grandmother was a teenager, three of her girlfriends were driving across the railroad tracks. A train struck the car, instantly killing the girls.

The three girls were buried in the Mission Trail Cemetery. Family members, as well as school friends, all heard the mournful wailing of a dog seeming to come from a wood-framed well on the cemetery grounds. They could see nothing down the well, but still, the wailing persisted until the services were over.

Afterwards, for any burial of a child, the eerie wailing could be heard, although no dog could be seen in the well or anywhere else.

Recently Kimberly visited the cemetery. A fence still surrounded it, and she found the gate chained and rusted shut. The entire area, slightly less than five acres large with only four having been used, was overgrown with weeds. One wonders if all family descendants have moved away, leaving no one to care for the graveyard behind rusted gates.

Plots are covered with wild grasses in the sandy acreage. Graves have sunk into the earth, and tombstones have fallen and broken.

In many instances only wooden or framed paper markers are staked by the graves, and many stones have no inscriptions remaining.

Several old cemeteries are still located in this general area, including the Concordia Cemetery in which several famous cowboys and outlaws of the old west are buried. This includes John Wesley Hardin, who reportedly killed forty-eight men. Other than that he was a nice enough gunslinger.

The Witch's Claw

To know the area of Redford, Texas, is to better understand the tale of the witch's claw. The prairies, desert, and mountains form a curious beauty. It has been that way for thousands of years.

According to historian Glenn Willeford, occasional torrential rainfalls blowing in from tropical disturbances in the Gulf of Mexico turn normally dry arroyos into raging demons that twist across the desert, destroying everything in their path.

Redford is located along the Rio Grande and Farm Road 170, more romantically known as "The Camino del Rio" (The River Road) in southern Presidio County.

In 1917 the U.S. Army established several posts in the area, including Marfa, Shafter, and Redford. The Great Depression did not excessively affect the county until 1932. Silver mines closed at Shafter, as we know from the tale *A Field of Crosses*.

This now brings us to our ghostly tale. The story came from the father of Enrique Madrid at Redford, to Glenn Willeford, to me ...and now to you. Such is the path of legends.

A cold winter night in 1933 found a group of Mexican-American men around a campfire. Not only did the fire warm them, but sipping *sotol*, a fiery native liquor, added to their comfort.

At a lull in conversation, they heard the thunk of a Rio Grande cowbell in the distance. The spooky sound caused at least one man to think of ghosts and cemeteries. Perhaps to relieve the boredom of the evening, he mentioned not one of them had the nerve to venture into the cemetery that night. His comment brought silence.

He then offered a suggestion. "Let us all put a coin into the pot, and if any one of you is brave enough to walk into the graveyard, he will earn the pot of coins."

The graveyard was about a half-mile southeast of town on a hill overlooking the Rio Grande. Someone in the group wondered how they would know the person really went there. They had to have a method for proof.

The first man said nothing, but strolled into a wooded area and brought back a cedar stake, sharpened at one end. He held it in front of the men. Whoever volunteered would take the stake and drive it into the grave of the *bruja* (a witch). Everyone knew the *bruja* lay just outside the hallowed ground of the graveyard.

They all looked at one another to see who would be the bravest.

Silence was broken by the sigh of one of the *vaqueros* who leaned against a tree. He lit a match, its glow illuminating his weathered face, adorned with a spindly mustache. He touched the flame to a hand-rolled cigarette and watched the thin spiral of smoke cut the frigid air.

Then he said, "I will do it. It is nothing." He took the stake and headed toward the graveyard. He wore an army overcoat, a relic of the U.S. Army's occupation of the border country from 1916 to 1920. The garment was long enough to drag the ground, and it had all the warmth a man needed on a wintry night.

The *vaqueros* watched for a while, continuing with their conversation and *sotol* until they ran out of both. They grew sleepy and decided to depart for their homes where they could rest in comfort.

Early the next morning, the man who thought of the idea in the first place decided to see if their friend had actually carried out the dare. He pulled his coat collar up around his face and left for the graveyard.

As soon as he arrived at the outer edge, he saw a pile of dark ragged cloth. It was at the head of the *bruja's* grave. Morning's light had not yet cut through the shadows, and he wasn't sure of what he saw. Then he recognized the coat of his friend. Was there a man beneath the ragged mound?

He stepped closer to the coat. Only when he kicked it to one side did he see the stake, driven deep into the *bruja's* grave. Through the coat!

The buttons were ripped off and the ground bore harsh divots as if dug out by boots of a terrified man. There was no sign of the *vaquero*. He may have managed to escape, but his coat remained.

Horrified, he had become the unsuspecting victim of the "witch's claw."

Cottonwood

The old Cottonwood graveyard is reminiscent of Mt. Pleasant Cemetery in East Texas. Someone is peering over your shoulder, and the cemetery is cold when it shouldn't be. That seems to be a universal comment about some graveyards, especially when something of a paranormal nature occurs.

When settlers, many of them German, arrived in southeastern Callahan County, they believed it to be close to "paradise." Native grasses and abundant wildlife made this land a good choice for farming and hunting.

J. W. Love originally settled in Cottonwood in the 1870s, eight miles northwest of Cross Plains. Farmers migrated from East Texas to Cottonwood because of the region's agricultural prospects, and soon the community became known as the area's leading trade center. And of course they had a cemetery, the next stop to paradise.

The town was also known for violence. Its main-street shootouts might possibly have something to do with the haunting of Cottonwood Cemetery. The suggestion of ghosts in Cottonwood is apparently so prolific, they might consider joining those in neighboring Taylor County.

It is said the air in Cottonwood Cemetery grows chilly on a warm day. It can be so quiet you can hear the silence. That is, until the wind begins to moan, then rushes past, causing you to wonder what it may carry within its grasp. At this point you realize the desolation you have entered. What makes you turn quickly when

Cottonwood Cemetery appears peaceful enough

your peripheral vision causes you to tingle? And you figure it isn't your allergy to cottonwood pollen.

This graveyard surrounded by a chain link fence is reached by a dirt road. An abandoned house stands nearby. The area is thick with trees inside and outside the graveyard. In order to read the stones, you might need to move away leaves and brush. Stones along the fence line may have been moved from the gravesite at an earlier date and never replaced. Other markers are broken.

The afternoon I visited this old graveyard, I saw no apparitions, captured no orbs on film. I felt a chill in the air—not all over, but in specific spots. My scheduled itinerary is to blame for the day visit.

Incidentally, a not-so-trivial trivia is Robert E. Howard, author of *Conan the Barbarian*, did much of his writing in Cross Plains. As far as I know, he never wrote a *Casper* cartoon.

One thing a friend commented on after a late night visit was the change in temperature from one section to the other—not to cold, but to much warmer. That was not the most important thing that occurred. As the group prepared to leave, a vaporous form seemed to race by a gravestone. An overactive imagination? They didn't think so.

Before leaving Cottonwood, are you sure you have your keys to the car? It's easy to lose things in Cottonwood Cemetery—even if it's only your nerve.

A Field of Crosses

The ghosts wander when the sun disappears behind the mountains. An old graveyard is the setting for wooden crosses, spaced apart with sufficient room for ghostly beings to walk. And if it were crowded, they would walk through them on their path to the stone fortress's remains in the mountains.

Only the ghosts seem to know who belongs where, as the crosses no longer have names. Any lettering has faded away. We can only speculate as to whom the graves belong.

But first it is necessary to know a little history of the ghost town of Shafter, where the white crosses stand. Once a booming silver town, Shafter rests on Cibolo Creek fifteen or twenty miles north of Presidio. This community in the desert didn't always rest.

Wealthy Milton Faver, known as the "Lord of Three Manors" by his Mexican workers, established the first Anglo-American ranch in Big Bend. In the 1850s he built his massive fort high in the mountains for protection against the Apaches.

Faver died in 1889, an old man with a long gray beard. He sleeps in his fort with the Apaches' mountains casting shadows; however, we don't know for a fact he sleeps peacefully. It is said he still wanders about in his former home.

The setting was created for ghosts.

History tells us Pascual Orozco Jr. spent time in the Shafter mountains. As a young man, he joined his father's business in

Mexico, and he did well. Be it through business or something more devious, he accumulated much gold and silver. "Stolen" might be more like it.

General Orozco, at the time of the Mexican Revolution, under direct orders from Huerta, commander of Federal forces, went north where he temporarily slowed Pancho Villa.

Villa, known by the people as a Mexican Robin Hood, the champion of the poor, did not leisurely spend his time in the area. He was either chasing forces or being chased. He moved through Shafter and Presidio, found Orozco, and shattered his forces. But Orozco escaped and charged back into town. Using part of his fortune, he paid off friends to protect him.

But what of the general's treasure? Legend says Orozco, having had much of his treasure with him, stashed the cache in an abandoned mineshaft in the mountains overlooking Shafter.

It is probable no one knows which mountain, the shaft's entrance long-since covered over with dirt and brush. Some wonder if the mine really ever existed. Others seem to think Villa found the treasure for the benefit of himself and his troops.

The town had seen so much activity and death, no wonder ghosts roam freely. The silver mines began playing out in the first decade of the 1900s, the same time of the Mexican Revolution.

Orozco escaped Shafter, only to get shafted from a posse who thought he was a bandit—so one story goes. He was buried as a general in Concordia Cemetery in El Paso, but his remains were later moved to Chihuahua. It is unlikely his spirit returned to Shafter. Then who knows, he may be back, looking for his gold.

Today, from Faver's fort, you can look up into the Apaches' mountains. Apache spirits are said to wander there around their own burial grounds. Whether or not they venture into the cemetery below, only they know. Unless of course you see their ghosts in Shafter, shafts of arrows at the ready as they ride war ponies down the mountainside to meet up with the phantoms of the wooden crosses.

Crinoline Petticoats and Cowboy Boots

nyone living in West Texas during the 1870s would have been certain the town of Belle Plain in Callahan County would thrive. It was written in the wind. Early on, three businesses were established, and by 1880 the community had the staggering population of 300 (the population was sober, the number was staggering). Eventually 1,000 people considered themselves Belle Plainers. A hotel and a newspaper, lawyers and doctors prospered.

Civic-minded citizens decided a grand college would lay the groundwork for their town to grow as large as San Angelo. Belle Plain was mainly on the Plain, but when the railroad went through it, no one would care. They had it made. Once established, the college became the higher learning institution in all West Texas. Many folks defined its success as the college of the future, offering languages, music, liberal arts, and science. Its main reputation came about through its music department.

The town's college boasted over a dozen grand pianos. Talented students attended the Methodist school built in 1884. Parents eagerly enrolled their offspring, never dreaming its revered doors would be closed before graduation.

The college offered more than an assortment of subjects. Instructors were the best available and discipline prevailed. According to author Nancy Robinson Masters, if students set foot in any of the town's saloons, they would be expelled from Belle Plain College forever.

The curriculum included social graces, and the school held parties, strictly chaperoned. Students looked forward to the school's special events in the spring. Singing and concerts became a regular feature of the music department, always drawing appreciative audiences.

About the time the college became firmly established, the writing in the wind came true. Wells ran dry in the surrounding area. Water had to be hauled in, at a price too high for its quality. The bitter drought of the late 1880s presented tragic results from which neither the town nor college could survive. To make matters worse, the railroad did not go through the town but was routed through Baird, six miles north.

The school closed its doors in 1892. Five years later only three or four families inhabited the little town.

Drive down County Road 295 and you will come to Belle Plain Cemetery. There are many gravesites there, some without markers and many with inscriptions worn away.

Belle Plain Cemetery

To see what is left of the town, continue on County Road 293 to 221. The remains include a couple of partial houses with chimneys standing.

A portion of the college remains. Even though it has historical markers, the school property is privately owned. The school made of stone was three stories high. A long hall runs through the middle of the building, with several rooms on each side—and lots of windows.

Count the cisterns! There are quite a few, with one close to the rear of the building, seeping water through the walls. The number of cisterns may be from the time of the drought when the school

Belle Plain College as it is today

was desperate for water. History tells us it didn't matter; the school would close.

How easy it would be to think apparitions of students might appear walking down the halls of Belle Plain College.

Would the music never again be heard? Should you decide to hear for yourself if it is silenced forever, drive out to the former college in the late evening. Pretend the streets are tree-lined and flowers bloom along the walkways. You may be fortunate to see young couples dancing to violin and piano accompaniment.

Girls wear pink dresses with crinoline petticoats, and young men wear their cowboy boots. Notice—the townsfolk may be observing along with you, smiling at the prosperity of their school and town.

Don't be disappointed when they disappear. It may be the school's curfew. Belle Plain College may briefly come alive any night when the moon is full.

The cemetery is nearby...maybe you see a ruffle of pink disappear.

"Follow Me!"

Hundreds of families moving westward in the 1800s buried loved ones along the way—perhaps beside the road with wooden crosses, never to be seen again by the grieving families.

Such a western route could have been along the San Saba River, where Camp San Saba was established in 1852. The military abandoned the fort a few years later, but several residents remained. After all, walls and a roof protected them from the elements, if not from the Indians. When the military reactivated the fort in 1868, under the name of Fort McKavett, the new community grew and accepted the name as its own.

Since military protection seemed no longer to be needed, in 1883, the troops again left the fort to whoever chose to live there. The small community and fort were located southwest of Menard, in Menard County. Wildflowers flourished and animal life was abundant. Settlers had their choice of white-tailed deer and squirrel, and their Thanksgiving tables did not lack for turkeys.

According to an oft-told legend and an article by Mary-Love Bigony, "In the Spirit," one of the spirits was the form of a young girl.

An event involving a family traveling west had tragic results. The incident supposedly occurred around 1905— with a four-year margin for error. That isn't exact, but who knows? The same incident apparently happened more than once.

The daughter had become ill before she and her family arrived at the fort. It isn't known for sure, but perhaps they had to take a detour to the only known place where they could find help for their dear child. Detours today can be a simple nuisance, but at that time, they could mean the difference in life or death. The family drove their wagon into the fort area, stopping for the night in one of the fort's old barracks.

We can visualize them now. The parents sat at their child's bedside as she grew weaker during the night. By morning the daughter had died. Having no choice, they buried her in the community's small cemetery. Saying their farewell prayers, the saddened family continued their journey, perhaps never to return.

That is not the end of the story. Several years later an abrupt knocking on their door awakened a couple living in the fort. Sleepy-eyed, the woman answered the door. At first she couldn't believe what she saw. Adjusting to the lamplight, she could see the visitor was a young girl. Her dress depicted an earlier time period, about 1905, with a slight margin for error.

The girl looked at the woman and said, "Follow me!"

Think a minute. What would *you* do? It doesn't matter from what era her clothes came. A girl stands at your door, faintly visible, demanding you follow her.

"Of course I'll follow you," you'd say. "Lead on!" Besides, she shouldn't be out so late without her parents.

It was to be expected, after putting on their shoes, that the husband accompanied his wife who accompanied their visitor. They picked up a lamp from the table and wondered as you are now, just where she planned to take them.

The girl's voice was distinct as they continued following her quickened pace. It is said she ran toward the barracks and once there, vanished into the wall. No one found a secret passage. She simply disappeared.

That night the couple looked for any evidence they might find of the young girl—a flower from her dress or a handkerchief. They found nothing, nor when day broke did they arrive at anything other than bewilderment.

It is said other people who lived in the community for many years after experienced similar occurrences. A girl apparently arose from her nearby grave and knocked on doors. Did she lead them to the old barracks room in which she died? Was she looking for her parents?

If you visit Fort McKavett for one of their tours, be watchful of a lithe figure scurrying from the cemetery toward the ruins of the fort.

Knock, knock!

Shafter Lake

You would have a difficult time locating Shafter Lake graveyard unless you had directions. There are no road markers to tell you how to find it. However, once you are near, perhaps the sounds of muffled rifle fire would alert you.

The town of Shafter Lake was actually on the shores of the lake, four miles west of Highway 385 in central Andrews County.

The sounds of muffled rifle fire can be heard here
Courtesy of Eric Archer

The bullet-riddled historical marker overlooking the lake lets us know a town once existed there: "First town in yet-unorganized Andrews County platted in 1908...Named for lake charted in 1875 survey of Colonel William R. Shafter whose maps and victories over powerful Indians opened the Permian Basin to settlement...."

In the mid-1800s Buffalo Soldiers were stationed at frontier forts and outposts from Texas to the Dakotas to help with the westward expansion of the United States. They were proud of the name the Indians had given them, as they knew the respect the Native Americans had for the buffalo.

Men eagerly enlisted and were paid thirteen dollars a month. That wasn't much, but it covered clothes, food, and shelter—sure to bring a better life.

Colonel Shafter and one of the units of Buffalo Soldiers with the 10th Cavalry were sent to the region in the 1870s to scout for Indians and to map sources of water when they discovered the lake around which the town would eventually be built.

Early in the 1900s two land developers promoted the alkaline lake and scrub brush as nothing less than paradise. People came from all over the northern United States to gain land. Shafter Lake was a bustling city all right and would surely become a boomtown. That was then. Not so in 1910. The citizens' dreams were short-lived. Once a disagreement began with nearby Andrews, the latter town won the bid for county seat. Shafter Lake rapidly declined.

That is the history.

This is the legend: A group of Buffalo Soldiers was ambushed in a ravine where the cemetery is now. It is believed by those who venture near the old graveyard that they can see vaporous shapes of Buffalo Soldiers wandering...like mustering ghosts. Are they looking for fallen comrades, or seeking those who ambushed them? It may be merely a re-enactment of their tragic ambush. They have only to glance across the way to see the Indian burial ground.

Shafter Lake Cemetery
Courtesy of Eric Archer

There is little remaining of the town except the old cemetery. The faded sign at the small graveyard reads "Shafter Lake Cemetery." A few names listed at the front gate are scarcely legible.

Ninety years after the exodus, Shafter Lake continues to draw the unsuspecting to its shores—people who have heard a lake is there. They look for a dock from which to release their boats. They won't find one.

If they wait until evening, they may hear the sound of muffled rifle fire.

Uno, Dos, Tres

Cristo Rey of the Sierra de Juarez Mountains, rising to a height of 4,576 feet above the dusty towns below, provides a stark yet suitable background for Smelter Cemetery. The cemetery is located near the river on the southwest side of El Paso, close to industrial Smeltertown on Interstate 10, U.S. Highway 80. Because of the lead the smelter had emitted, the city tried to evacuate Smeltertown in the mid-1970s. The idea didn't go over so well with the townspeople, but for health reasons, they were finally forced to leave.

Should you decide to visit the cemetery, be prepared to drive up a steep dirt road through piles of coal and rubble, to the top of a dusty plateau. The gate is clearly marked.

Paper and silk flowers, wreaths, and crosses decorate the predominately Mexican cemetery. Graves are covered with large flat rocks or concrete slabs, mainly to discourage wild animals. However, a tradition was to cover the graves with mounds of rocks.

Native vegetation takes the place of planted shrubbery in many desert cemeteries, but the areas come alive with wild flowers in the spring. Well, perhaps not everything comes alive.

Smelter Cemetery
Courtesy of Kimberly Olsen

Kimberly Olsen, an active member of the El Paso chapter of Southwest Paranormal Investigators, tells us the reasons why in more than one way:

Uno. Railroad tracks, parallel to most of the road, border one side of the cemetery only a few dozen yards from its gate.

Kimberly says the cemetery has a really forgotten feel to it. Her uncle, a veteran of the El Paso Police Department, heard many reports of a crying woman seen walking these tracks. One report might not have been seen as important, but after sightings continued, people began taking the careworn woman seriously.

When investigators responded, the woman vanished into the cemetery. As the story goes, a train on these tracks had killed the poor woman's entire family. The reason for her wandering has yet to be answered, but some have surmised she is searching for anyone who may have survived.

Dos. Mt. Cristo Rey looms above El Paso at the point where Texas, New Mexico, and Mexico meet. On the summit, a massive monument of Jesus Christ stands, a difficult climb people are warned to attempt only in groups. Many years ago, Kimberly's father climbed the peak on a pilgrimage. As he climbed, he witnessed strange bright colored lights in the sky. They were not from planes, reflections from the town, or from any traffic down below. The mystery remained unexplained.

Tres. Even though Kimberly and her mother, Joyce Olsen, had visited Smelter before, they returned to take new photographs.

As in early Catholic cemeteries, wooden and iron crosses are found on many gravesites. The wooden crosses were painted white or left natural. Sometimes they staked, but more often they were placed in cement atop the graves. In many cases they had no inscriptions but not because they had worn away. According to Terry Jordan, author of *Texas Graveyards*, in frontier times, burial records identifying each gravesite were kept in the church.

On the occasion of Kimberly's recent photography session, she focused on the scene with the mountains in the background. As she aimed, a weathered cross in the viewfinder began to tilt. With a loud creak, it moved about ten inches just before she clicked the shutter.

A tilted cross
Courtesy of Kimberly Olsen

Kimberly said she could have jumped out of her skin. And who could blame her? She felt the urge to straighten the cross. It was not as if it pulled in the opposite direction, but in trying to straighten it, she could scarcely define the strange feeling that came over her. Even though the temperature was about 75 degrees, the wood felt cold and oily. She was glad to release it and return to her car.

Many of the crosses have deteriorated, with only mounds of dirt and rock to assert graves had ever been there at all. Whose remains rest in the unmarked graves? Many children of course, loved ones of long ago, and perhaps soldiers from early Fort Bliss. To visit Smelter after dark might provide an explanation.

Then again, it may be best to leave some questions unanswered.

Concordia

Most western states had a "Boot Hill" cemetery, and Texas was one of them. El Paso's Concordia Cemetery had once been called by that name.

Over 65,000 gravesites, including fifteen sections, cover Concordia. Now that's a lot of boots, including those of John Wesley Hardin. Hardin, son of a circuit-riding Methodist preacher and

65,000 plots and the Franklin Mountains
Courtesy of Kimberly Olsen

named after the founder of Methodism, considered himself a pillar of society who killed to save his own life. If this were so, he escaped death at least thirty times. However he did spend fifteen years in prison for murder.

After receiving a pardon, Hardin passed a law examination and opened an office in El Paso. By this time he probably already knew enough about the law not to *need* an examination. His newfound career was short-lived. Three months after putting up his shingle, he took a bullet in the back.

Hardin's grave is outlined with a single row of flat red stones. A red flower is consistently placed at his gravesite . . . placed there by whom? Reports allege that a Spanish lady has been seen mourning near his grave. It is possible she left the flower. It could also be possible she is an apparition. Nevertheless, a flower is there.

John Wesley Hardin and the mysterious flower
Courtesy of Kimberly Olsen

With so many gravesites, more than one haunting is apt to turn up. A commercial business is adjacent to one section of Concordia

Cemetery. Kimberly Olsen stopped inside to ask if anyone knew of possible hauntings in Concordia. They seemed reluctant to talk about it; however, as she was leaving, one employee spoke to her. He said his cousin had quit his job after hearing voices coming from the graveyard.

Cribs and baby beds seem to be a tradition in many graveyards, whether the graveyards are old or new. "Beds" are often found in far West Texas cemeteries.

One particular crib at the site of a baby's grave in Concordia is painted white with pink trim. It is a touching scene—a white cross attached to the head of the little crib. Placed inside the framework, a cluster of pink flowers fills a small vase next to an angel statue and small toys.

El Paso Haunted Trolley reports this gravesite of a cribdeath to show haunted activity. Every year on the anniversary of death there is a sighting of white balls of light, which emerge from the "crib." This grave is surrounded by other babies who all died very close to the same time. There is a bit of a white haze at the foot of the crib.

Courtesy of Kimberly Olsen

Every year on the anniversary of the baby's death, there is a sighting of white balls of light coming from the crib. This sighting has been reported by the "Haunted Trolley" tour guide.

El Paso has a bus system in which the buses are modified to look like trolley cars, and they service the downtown area. A "Haunted Trolley" offers tours to haunted sites in El Paso, as well as to Juarez, just across the border.

If you take this tour and the seat next to you *appears* to be vacant, don't rush when you get up. You might trip over a ghost.

Long Tom March

The exact location of this small West Texas graveyard is unknown. It has no doubt disappeared like tumbleweeds on the prairie. Still, you might look for any remaining gravestones on a desolate plot of land somewhere close to Abilene in Taylor County.

According to Charles Edwin Price, folklore collector and Southern historian, the ghost of "Long Tom" March roams the area in which he was buried in the late 1800s.

It seems Long Tom had a vice and maybe more than one. Chances are, gambling did him in. Now I wasn't there and neither was anyone else still above ground, but ol' Tom liked his liquor and he liked to play poker.

The town where he lived—the one now turned to dust— surely had a livery stable, general store, a hotel of sorts, and yes, a house of pleasure. The latter would have ranked a close second to the saloon.

Long Tom possessed a notorious reputation for exhibiting a hair-trigger temper. To prove it, he had several notches on his six-gun and one or two on his Bowie knife. Poker rated as his favorite indoor sport. He was adamant about winning and got plumb miffed when he lost. As a matter of fact, even when he lost he insisted he won. Therefore, his opponents had undoubtedly cheated. Rarely did anyone argue with him.

As is the case with someone who always gets away with something, Long Tom never thought he would meet a man who took offense to his temperament. Live and let fall dead if it suited the occasion. One day Tom must have carried his self-confidence a little too far.

That time the person he accused of cheating held his ground. He also held his gun. Being faster with his weapon, the man let Long Tom have a bullet right between the eyes. This shot didn't give him a heavy percentage for recovery. He died on the way to the floor, a long way down considering his height.

It could not be said the little community shed too many tears over Long Tom's death. He was carried to boot hill or wherever and buried with not a lot of remorse.

The killer received no punishment for the deed—possibly gratitude, but no punishment.

The story was not over. Tom's penchant for having the last word, or the last winning hand, was still in effect.

It is said Long Tom ascends from his grave when darkness falls, a deck of cards in hand. The very night after they buried Long Tom March, several people vowed they saw a thin gaunt figure walking down the main street. Okay, it was the only street. Darkness had already covered the town, but the men were sure it was Long Tom coming towards them. As they got closer to the figure, it disappeared.

Not that the townsfolk *really* believed in ghosts, but they still found their mounts and took a little ride to the graveyard. The site looked the same as when they lowered Long Tom into the soil the previous day. It was packed down, already dried out from the blowing winds. It didn't look as if anyone had dug his way out, and besides, there was that hole in his head. All that blood, remember?

However, the following night a familiar figure strode through the batwing doors of the saloon and sat alone at a corner table. He began shuffling a deck of cards, as he had done many times before, and waited for someone to join him for poker—just a friendly game.

The bartender stopped swiping out the glasses with a bar rag and leaned his arms on the counter. He stared at the lone man at the table then beckoned another customer over to the bar. He asked him who he thought the cowboy was. The man, who probably had one too many already, quickly ordered another whiskey and downed it in one gulp, saying nothing.

That gave the bartender his answer. He laid down the rag then cleared his throat and walked over to the table. He looked straight at the cowboy, ready to find out what was going on. Long Tom's twin, perhaps? As soon as he got within five feet of the table, the figure vanished in a mist.

The ghost of Long Tom could be seen many times after that night. He might just wander around the graveyard or sometimes down the street, always with his cards. Occasionally he came into the saloon, but when he did, other customers did the vanishing act.

When the town's population moved in closer to Abilene and surrounding communities, the former's businesses closed up, including the saloon. Long Tom never left. His spirit continued to wander, looking for a good game of poker. Any game he could win was a good game.

In your travels around Abilene, if you happen to see a silhouette of a tall lean man carrying a deck of cards out on the prairie, go ahead and stop.

Long Tom March might even be sociable . . . as long as you let him win.

Chapter 12

The Last Word

Tombstones

Depending on the economical status of the family, more elaborate or personally designed markers have come into fashion as years passed. The mode of transportation on the way to the final destination has also changed.

The National Museum of Funeral History in Houston is home of rare artifacts and historical information about one of our most important cultural rituals. The museum houses the country's largest display of funeral memorabilia in its over 20,000 square feet.

Included in early traditional forms of funereal transportation is a gold-adorned horse-drawn carriage, as well as early hearses such as were used in Texas. On display are funeral service vehicles, still operable today.

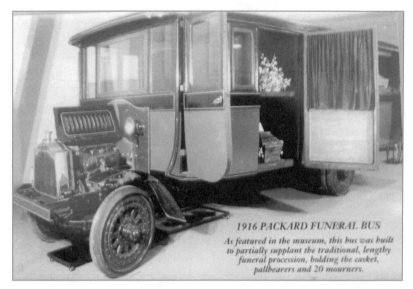

1916 PACKARD FUNERAL BUS

As featured in the museum, this bus was built to partially supplant the traditional, lengthy funeral procession, holding the casket, pallbearers and 20 mourners.

Early Texas Burial Traditions, *1916 Packard Funeral Bus*
Courtesy Gary Sanders, National Funeral Museum

This funeral bus was built to replace lengthy and traditional funeral processions. It held the casket, flowers, pallbearers, and as many as twenty mourners. The vehicle may have been the first chartered bus. It has been reported that when climbing a hill, the short-lived bus tipped backward. Pallbearers tumbled over the mourners, and the casket turned over.

An 18-Wheeler

A trucker who apparently loved his eighteen-wheeler, took a replica of it with him. This memorable marker is in a Grand Saline cemetery.

D.C. White facing south

D. C. White's present marker in Canton is a replacement of an earlier one carved in rock. No, he wasn't a horse thief, or at least he wasn't tried for that. A jury found him guilty of murdering George Conquest. In 1966 Ira Murphrey made the headstone to replace the one that had become illegible. This marker is the only one facing south in the cemetery, the custom for outlaws and other bad guys.

A "decent" monument

In the 1887 will of one of my ancestors, he asked that $1,000 be spent on his monument. "If that is not enough, add more. I want it done decent."

Raggedy Ann and Andy
Courtesy of Carol Stavlo

In an Amarillo cemetery, these markers stand at the graves of two children.

✧✧✧

A Mourning Woman

A wife was so saddened by the death of her husband in 1977, she commissioned an Italian artist to sculpt a figure of a mourning woman. The life-size figure depicting the woman's grief was placed by her husband's grave in a Memphis cemetery. Charlotte Boykin Carlson died in 1999 and now rests between her husband Reuben Carlson and the "other woman."

Scarecrow Lady
Courtesy of Jen Fenter

This friendly wooden scarecrow-lady marks the grave of Jarrice I. Shone (February 1, 1938 - March 16, 1994). Hanging on the pole by her side is a decorative birdfeeder. The headstone's pediment is etched with hearts. The large tree with its shading branches creates a comfortable setting. It might be accurate to say Jarrice Shone spent much time in the outdoors. Chances are, she made a point to leave seed for the birds, and whoever knew that carried out her wish.

✧✧✧

A musical tribute
Courtesy of Billie Hallmark Mills

A Tyler piano teacher preplanned her monument—a full-size marble baby grand piano. So far, no one has reported hearing melodious cadences of familiar music coming from Rose Hill Cemetery.

Epitaphs

After the Revolution, stonecutters kept ledgers with their designs, so family members could easily choose an appropriate symbol for their loved one. Elaborate heart-wrenching epitaphs often marked monuments of the dead.

Messages, as if meant for the departed to read, were engraved in aged stone. Framed daguerreotypes were often embedded in them, and we can still see photographs of loved ones in cemeteries across the state.

Our ancestors probably thought engraved stones would last forever. The surface wears away via an assortment of causes: rain, wind, sand. In overgrown graveyards, with the passage of time, twining poison ivy can wear into the marker's surface. Rainwater contains a certain acid that can destroy limestone.

Often stones are knocked over by fallen trees or by vandals. Today's markers frequently have only the name and dates of the departed. In early times epitaphs were more detailed, with complete dates and a little family history.

In Oakwood Cemetery in Tyler, Texas, a genealogist would be delighted at the foresight of the family of Martha Virginia Boon. Her husband's stone was similarly marked, including his birthplace of Williamson County, Tennessee:

> Martha Virginia Boon
> Wife of John A. Boon
> Born Dec. 14, 1839
> Married November 22, 1866
> Died in Tyler July 2, 1895
>
> Here in this spot where Christians sleep
> Oh why do we in anguish weep?
> They are not lost but gone before
> God knows best
> Not my will but Thine O Lord
>
> Nearer my God to thee nearer to thee
> There let the way appear steps into Heaven
> In the sweet by and by
> O how sweet
> I have lived for this hour.

A monument in Smith County's Oakwood Cemetery is imposing by its size as well as the story that goes with it. On Memorial Day of 1807, the Daughters of the Confederacy arranged a celebration in Tyler's Town Square. School bands played in the area. In the square, people set up tables from which to serve the great amounts of food. They placed picnic tablecloths on the ground. A fine day proceeded with the people participating feeling a great surge of patriotism.

After the meal and music, three thousand participants walked or rode buggies out to the cemetery, no short distance, where the monument was dedicated.

Erected by Mollie Mode Davis Chapter
Daughters of the Confederacy
By popular
Subscription
A.D. 1907

In tender
Reverence of the
Memory of soldiers
From Smith County who Fought
In the Armies of the Confederacy.

In Hood County, Asbury Cemetery:

No pain, no grief, no anxious fear
Can reach the peaceful sleeper here.

In Aurora Cemetery in Wise County, a child's sad epitaph:

I was so soon done, I don't know why I was begun.

Greenwood Cemetery in Parker County:

BOSE IKARD

Served with me four years on the Goodnight-
Loving Trail. Never shirked
A duty or disobeyed an order.
Rode with me in many stampedes,
Participated in three engagements with the
Comanches. Splendid behavior.

— Charles Goodnight

In Elmwood Memorial Park in Abilene:

Those who care will surely know.

In Union Cemetery, Comanche County:

To live in the hearts
We leave behind
Is not to die

Mills Cemetery, Dallas County:

1881-1891

Parents good night, my work is done.
I go to rest with the setting sun,
but not to wake with the morning light,
so dear Parents a long good night.

A Kirbyville, Texas, version of the New England epitaph:

Behold my grave as you pass by
Where you are now, so once was I
Where I am now You soon shall be
Prepare for death and follow me

In Van Zandt County, a 1947 stone reads:

"Goodhearted woman in love with her good timing man"

For those Whose Dear Love   My rainy day woman
I did rise and fall   My wife
My love, My husband   Loving Mom, Loving Grandma

Crown Hill Cemetery in Dallas County:

BONNIE PARKER

As the flowers are all made sweeter by
the sunshine and the dew, so this old
world is made brighter by the lives
of folks like you.

(No offense, Bonnie indeed made Texas more colorful.)

San Jose Burial Park, San Antonio:

HELOISE

Every Housewife's Friend
-30-

The following is from a cemetery in South Texas:

In her life she was a pattern to be followed and her death—
Oh! How consoling to her friends.

After the name of the departed:

The deceased left two daughters—both girls.

I often wonder if some of the epitaphs we hear about are true.
Such as:

He was young, he was fair.
But the Injuns raised his hair.

At least descendants would know how their ancestor died!

Is Jesse really buried in Missouri? Rumor has it he is buried in
Texas. He possibly is, but not necessarily in North Texas as many
people think.

Jesse James
Kearney, Missouri

Died April 3, 1882
Aged 34 years, 8 months, 28 days
Murdered by a traitor and a coward
whose name is not worthy
to appear here.

The following are not Texans, but who could resist including them:

Edgar Allen Poe

"Quoth the Raven Nevermore"

Dean Martin

"Everybody Loves Somebody Sometime"

Johnny Yeast

"Here lies Johnny Yeast
Pardon me for not rising."

✧✧✧

If you want to be remembered in a certain way, write your own epitaph in your will. This is your chance to have the last word. Elaborate or not, if anyone talks back to you, you won't have to listen.

~ May the spirits rest in peace ~

Sources

Magazines/Brochures/Articles

Newstand, "In the Spirit," Mary-Love Bigony, Oct. 1988

Texas Co-op Power, "The Most Haunted Town in Texas," Lisa Farwell, Oct. 2000

"Buried in Texas," Carol Rust, Aug. 4, 1996

Newspapers

Abilene Reporter-News, "Debate continues over presence of ghosts at Fort Phantom," Brian Bethel, Oct. 31, 1998

Abilene Reporter-News, "Fort Phantom Hill," Bobby Horecka, Aug. 1, 1999

American Statesman, "Texas prison may be truest haunted house of all," Mike Ward, Oct. 28, 1999

Arlington Citizen-Journal, Katrina Williams, Aug. 21, 1988

Athens Review, "Seeking lost parks, pentagrams," Brian Spurling, Athens, TX, Nov. 1989

Bowie News

Corpus Christi Caller Times, "Chipita's execution haunted local memory," Feb. 2, 1998

The Dallas Morning News, "Tolbert's Texas," Frank X. Tolbert, May 15, 1983

The Dallas Morning News, "Proper Burial," Diane Jennings, June 1999

East Texas Journal, "Blue Light story linked to Barrett Cemetery," Hudson Old, publisher, May 1998

Fort Worth Star-Telegram, "Urban legends: Arlington lore leaves lasting impressions," Abbi Hertz, Oct. 18, 1998

Fort Worth Star-Telegram, "Historic Thurber down, not out," Bill Fairley, Mar. 23, 2001

The Mabank Monitor, "Vendor prepares his own casket," Kathryn Culver and Connie Lee, April 30, 2000

Memphis Democrat

Monahan News, "Pascual Orozco Jr.," May 1, 1977
Monahan News, "Top Stories," May 1, 1997
Pecos Enterprise
The Purity Crusade, E. M. Dealy, Jan. 1921
San Antonio Express News—"Sunday Magazine," Dustin
    Coleman, Oct. 1989
The Springtown Epigraph
Texas Monthly, "Genial Jefferson," Virginia B. Wood
The Weekly Gazette of Fort Worth, July 1, 1887

Online
Big Bend Travel Information
City of Plano, Texas Official Web Site
City of the Silent, "Cemetery Symbolism" by Joel GAzis-SAx
Dagulf's Ghost
The Handbook of Texas
Family Tree Maker's Genealogy Site
Lone Star Spirits
Shadowlands
Texas Parks and Wildlife: Exploring Texas "Ghosts of the
    Prairie"
The Handbook of Texas
The Healer of Los Olmos, Ruth Dodson
Virtual Texan Ghost Forum
www.texasescapes.com

Books
All My Downs Have Been Ups, Nancy Robinson Masters,
    MasAir Publications, 1992-1998
The Best of Texas Folk and Folklore, Ruth Dodson, University of
    North Texas Press, 1954, 1998
The Black Hope Horror, Ben and Jean Williams, William Morrow
    and Company, 1991

Corpses, Coffins, and Crypts, Penny Colman, Henry Holt and
  Company, 1997
Daddy Said, Elvis Allen, Legacy Publishing Company, 1999
The Folk Healer, Eliseo Torres, University of North Texas
  Press, 1954, 1998
Encyclopedia Britannica
The Folk Healer, Eliseo Torres, Nieves Press
Footprints Along the Border, William Gwaltney
Galloping Ghosts, Betty Jo Clendenin, Clendenin Books, 1997
Ghost Stories of Old Texas, Zinita Fowler, Eakin Press, 1983
Ghost Stories of Texas, Ed Syers, Texian Press, 1981
National Directory of Haunted Places, Dennis William Hauck,
  Althamor Press, 1994
Phantoms of the Plains, Docia S. Williams, Republic of Texas
  Press, 1996
Riverport to the Southwest, Fred Tarpley, Eakin Press, 1985
Tales That Must Not Die, Juan Sauvageau, Oasis Press, 1975,
  1984
Texas Tales Your Teacher Never Told You, Charles Eckhardt,
  Wordware Publishing, 1992
Van Zandt County Cemetery Book #4, LaVonna Blackwell,
  Editor
Wood County Cemeteries, Vol. 1 & 2

Letters
Author's letter collection of Great-Grandmother Permelia
  Nickell Hawkins

Libraries, Museums, Genealogical Societies
Bowie Public Library
Kaufman County Library
National Museum of Funeral History, Houston
Oldham County Library in Vega
Red River Historical Museum, Sherman

Special Collections Division, University of Texas at Arlington
Libraries
Van Zandt County Genealogical Society
Wood County Library

Individuals Who Graciously Offered Information for Stories
Mark Angle, Lee Angle Photography, Inc., Fort Worth
Eric Archer, Odessa
Linda Archer, Odessa
Ann Arnold, author, Fort Worth
Wallace Bennett, *Cottonwood News*, *Cross Plains Review*,
Cottonwood
Virginiae Blackmon, Fort Worth
Christine Bozarth, Bowie
Mary Jo Clendenin, author, Stephenville
Shelly Cross, Hutchinson County Museum, Borger
Karla McKinney DeCluette, Fort Worth
Nichole Dobrowloski, historical investigator-documentalist,
Ghost of Fort Bend County, Sugar Land
Linda-Jeanne Dolby, historian, Garland
Kelly Ehlinger, nurse/paralegal, Pearland
Jen Fenter, Cedar Creek
Ray and Marcia Fisher
Chris Garcia, Houston
Blake Harris, Jefferson
Carolyn Haviland, media coordinator, Lone Star Spirits
Peter Haviland, lead investigator, Lone Star Spirits
Bob Hopkins, Weatherford
Kathey Kelley Hunt, cemetery preservationist, Kaufman
Mark Jean, Ghoststalkers of Texas, Fort Worth
Christina Kidd, Houston
Charles LaFon, Bowie
Jack Loftin, historian, Windthorst

Nancy Robinson Masters, author, Abilene

Jason McIntosh

Dr. Devon Mihesuah, author, professor, editor of *American Indian Quarterly*, University of Northern Arizona

Chris Moseley, parapsychologist, Mabank

Joyce Irelene Olsen, sales manager, El Paso

Kimberly Olsen, Southwest paramormal investigator, El Paso

Terry Patrick, L.V.N./R.N., El Paso

Katie Phillips, administrator/webmaster, Lone Star Spirits

David Place, Harlingen

Charles Edwin Price, author and Southern folklorist

Cindi Rawlings

Cindy Ritcheson, genealogist, Arlington

Aimee Robison, Merkel

Marcia K. Rolbiecki, Red River Historical Museum, Sherman

Gary Sanders, curator, National Museum of Funeral History, Houston

Brockman Smith, Arp

Brian Spurling, Athens

Carol Stavlo, Lubbock

Jade Stone, Mt. Pleasant

Robyn Street, For McKavett State Historical Park

Peggye Swenson, author, Cleburne

John Troesser, editor, www.texasescapes.com, Fayetteville

Glenn Willeford, historian, Chihuahua, Mexico

Ralph Wranker, "armature historian," Kingsville

Contacts

Linda Andrews, Collin County Community College, Frisco

Christine Brockman, Chamber of Commerce, Albany

Mabel Cook, Van Zandt County Genealogy Society, Canton

Jon Dews, Tyler

Larry Francell, Director, Museum of the Big Bend, Alpine

Sources

Jackie Hawkins, Fort Worth
Tony Hawkins, Fort Worth
John Klingman, Curator of Exhibits, Museum of the Big Bend,
    Alpine
Amber McClendon, Grace Museum, Abilene
Peggy McCracken, Webmaster, *Pecos Enterprise*
Cleo Moss, Fort Worth
Patty F. Priddy, Sugar Land
Patsy Vinson, Van Zandt County Genealogy Society, Canton

Photographs
All photographs were taken by Olyve Hallmark Abbott unless otherwise noted.

Index